T0196120

WHO IS MY
Neighbour?

JOHN CHRISTIE

authorHOUSE®

AuthorHouse™ UK
1663 Liberty Drive
Bloomington, IN 47403 USA
www.authorhouse.co.uk
Phone: 0800.197.4150

Published by AuthorHouse 02/06/2017

ISBN: 978-1-5246-7667-4 (sc)
ISBN: 978-1-5246-7666-7 (hc)
ISBN: 978-1-5246-7668-1 (e)

Print information available on the last page.

This book is printed on acid-free paper.

Cover illustrated by Roger Eburne.

Dedication and thanks

"To my wife for her love, encouragement and editorial assistance."

Chapter 1

George Meredith is in his BMW series 5 car driving to his current residence in Blackpool. This is not his permanent home. That is a bachelor pad in Manchester and it is used as a bolt hole from whatever relationship he is escaping. But today George is heading for the home of Mrs. Cynthia Reynolds and feeling quite satisfied with himself. He is in a good set-up. Christmas is only a week away and he is looking forward to spending most of it in bed with Cynthia and the rest of it eating and drinking at her expense.

George does not have a steady job – in fact he despises anyone who has such a mundane way of life. Such people are suckers, dimwits who have no imagination and less intelligence.

George's way and view of life is that he does people favours. In particular he does favours for single ladies – preferably young to middle aged and, essentially, with independent means. In other words they should be favoured both physically and financially. George knows that he is attractive to women. Just under six feet tall with dark curly hair which he arranges in careless disorder, over his ears and just covering his collar at the back of his neck. He dresses casually but expensively – a fact that rarely misses attention.

He knows that his way of life is not approved by many – indeed, it is essentially criminal. George is aware of this but does not regard himself as a criminal. By befriending ladies who are alone he gives them affection and, he believes, satisfactory sex. If they repay their gratitude by lending him money to expand his business, which incidentally does not exist except as a creation of his imagination, he regards that as being his just reward. When he finally leaves his temporary love nest, he does so just as his lady friend is becoming bored with him or is getting suspicious about his activities or lack of them. He has so far been able to sense when the tide of suspicion has started to turn. Up until his last encounter, George has seen the writing on the wall early, well before the relationship deteriorates into confrontation. He usually gets out of the situation by inventing an email from foreign parts demanding his immediate presence. Then, like Aeneas of old leaving his Dido, he will "silence her mourning with words of returning but never intending to visit her more."

The only financial problem with this life is that it requires investment principally in clothes, cars and in purchasing drinks and meals as a means of establishing a relationship. George's usual method is to find a suitable lady by frequenting hotels bars and up-market pubs. Here he listens to conversations and tries to home in upon what he hopes will be a fruitful target.

George does have an additional source of income. From his teens he has been keen on horse racing and over the years has developed an expertise. He rarely bets on the favourite or second favourite, but always checks the form of his horses on their last few outings over the ground conditions. So he places his bets on medium odds and only for a place in the first three or four in a race. His wins all tend to be at small margins but cumulatively they give him a steady income. Only rarely will he place a long-odds bet when he thinks he has inside information. He also never bets more than four or five hundred pounds in a day and never tries to offset a loss by doubling his bets. Thus he makes at least enough to pay his occasional hotel costs when he is obliged to stay in one and all other day to day living costs. In addition, he is putting sufficient aside for his master plan. Finally, as a fall-back residence, he has a small bachelor flat on the outskirts of Manchester which, by steadily increasing in price, is also a useful investment.

Another occupation of George is to visit sports or fitness centres. He prides himself on his physique which is always admired by his lovers and for good reason. His muscular arms and legs and the ridged, 6-pack stomach muscles always provoke admiration and he actually enjoys the effort he puts in on the treadmill and the weights. Such activities do not count as work. Sports centres are also a useful pick-up places for young women who like their sex to be a fight rather than a surrender. George prefers it that way as well. He is surprisingly strong for his slim build.

Indeed, it is in one such place that he met Cynthia. Having a cooling drink in the sports centre café after a strenuous session with weights, he was impressed by the arrival of a well-built lady, perhaps in her mid-thirties. Dressed in tight-fitting lycra, she possessed a tightly muscled rear end and a spectacular pair of breasts. George casually watched her out of the corner of his eye as she walked up to the service counter but his full attention was attracted by an exclamation of "Damn!. I've no money in my purse."

In exasperation she turned away from the counter and then spotted George.

"Is there anyone here would like to buy a poor girl a drink?" she asked coyly addressing her remarks to no-one in particular. However, there was no mistaking to whom she was talking and George laughed.

"It'll be a pleasure. What will it be?"

With the drink bought, introductions were made and soon they were genuinely enjoying each other's company and getting to know one another. To George this meeting was extremely fortuitous especially once he learned of Cynthia's divorce status and generous divorce settlement.

To attract attention, George has learned that he must appear to be wealthy. If the relationship gets past the idle chat stage to dinner engagements and perhaps sleeping arrangements, then George has to put his hand in his pocket. As the cliché puts it, he must speculate in order to accumulate. A flash car is an absolute necessity. So George's next step was to invite Cynthia to dinner the following evening. The date was readily accepted along with the offer to pick up from Cynthia's house.

One of the precautions which George has taken to prevent being followed or identified is to have spare number plates for his car. He has bought his BMW on a hire purchase scheme which has involved a minimal down payment. Then he has, almost round the first corner, swapped the number plates over to new ones, of which he has several sets obtained illegally from a garage owning friend. When he drives off into the sunset he is confident that he will never be detected even if it means allowing his hair to grow and sporting a light beard. Over the years, George has accumulated substantial sums which he has secreted in various bank accounts under different names. To go with these he has credit cards and debit cards. However, he usually exists on one of these accounts only - what he thinks of as his working capital. His main capital reserves are in a bank in Barcelona where he hopes to retire once he has enough to buy an apartment in the south of Spain and continue the life of a single gent amongst female holiday makers – thus continuing his present way of life but in better weather.

Rarely had George's approaches been so readily accepted and the following evening George ended up in Cynthia's bed. After an energetic and enjoyable night, George received an invitation to move in for the foreseeable future. George could scarcely believe his good fortune and as he returns to his love-nest this evening he has a self-satisfied smirk on his face. In fact, he is so pleased with himself that, were it not for the fact that he is driving along at sixty miles per hour, he would be rubbing his hands together with glee.

Part of George's fictitious background has been the production of a business card from an imaginary business which gives him the position of Managing Director of Innovative Developments Limited with a postal address in nearby Fleetwood, telephone number and email address.

This evening when George returns from his non-existent hard day at the office Cynthia displays a quite different side to her personality. He advances into the front sitting room for his usual kiss but stops when Cynthia stands in front of him with arms folded and, George notices, his suitcase at her feet. George does not need a crystal ball to detect that there is trouble in store.

"I've spent an interesting day," said Cynthia, holding him at arm's length.

"What would that be then?" replied George sensing a distinct cooling of the atmosphere.

Cynthia holds up George's business card.

"You bastard!" she screeches. "I know what your game is. Into my bed and then into my wallet. Do you really think I'm that stupid? That I wouldn't check on your address and telephone?"

George attempted to speak.

"Just get out!" she yells. She picks up George's suitcase and throws it at his head. Being very fit from her sports centre activities it comes with considerable force and strikes him painfully on the cheek.

If she expects George to turn and sneak away like a beaten dog, she is mistaken. George does not like this treatment and shows his own short fuse. He reacts quickly and violently in the manner learned from his street fighting background where you had to finish the job quickly and decisively or get badly beaten.

"You bitch!" He punches her viciously in the stomach and as she collapses forward, totally winded, he brings his knee up to meet her full in the face. The head moving downward at speed meeting a knee moving up at the same speed doubles the energy absorbed by the skull and hence the brain. Her head snaps back and she collapses to the floor.

"Bitch" he mutters again.

The woman has plainly been knocked unconscious. George rubs his knee and looks more closely at her. Her breathing seems quite erratic and, even as he watches, it falters and then with a rattle stops and a trickle of blood dribbles from her mouth.

"Fuck, fuck, fuck," says George and stands stunned for a minute. He had hit her hard but surely, he thinks, not hard enough to kill. He checks her breathing and neck pulse but can detect nothing. She is dead.

The enormity of what he has done quickly occurs to him and with it a sinking feeling in the pit of his stomach. In a brief moment, he suddenly sees looming in front of him a new future – a move from petty criminal at worst to a serious criminal who can expect a long prison sentence. He feels sick and dashing to the downstairs toilet vomits into the lavatory. Feeling weak he leans against the wall and starts to think about what he must do.

His first inclinations is to get out of the house as soon as possible. To run as far and as fast as he can. However, he then realises that if he leaves things as they are, even with the most optimistic outlook, it will not be assessed as an accidental death. It will not take long for the probable perpetrator to be identified and there would only be one suspect in the frame.

"Fuck, fuck, fuck," mutters George again.

His first constructive thought is to make the death look accidental. The blow to her face could have been caused by a fall down the stairs, he figures, and so his first task is to drag the body to the foot of the stairs and that has to be done quickly. His knowledge of sudden deaths, gleaned from the crime fiction which is his preferred reading, is that movement of a body after death can be detected by the way in which the blood of the victim settles at the lowest point of the body. Therefore, he has to position the body as it now lies.

George half lifts, half drags the dead body out from the sitting room where the confrontation had occurred to the foot of the stairs and arranges the body more or less as it had been. He then goes back over his tracks and flattens out where the dragged foot has scraped the carpet. So far, so good.

His next thought is that his punch to the stomach may be detectable in any post mortem examination and he puzzles over this for some time. Then he has a brainwave. If she had been carrying something heavy, she could have tripped and in falling, and it could have hit her in the midriff. He fixes upon a small table which she used either in her bedroom or in the sitting room. It is heavy and awkward. Gripping it only on the edges using the palms of his hands, he retrieves it from the bedroom and takes it to the foot of the stairs. There he smashes one leg of it against the floor then leaves the table upside down beside the body.

Next comes the question of fingerprints. His first thought is to wipe over everything he might have touched during his short stay in the house but he reckons that if the police think there was anything suspicious about the "accident", the absence of prints would confirm that view. Better to leave that alone and take himself off immediately. If he is followed up he will say that the accident must have happened after he had left. The important thing is to not leave any grounds for doubt and he feels he has done that. At least he knows his prints will not be on any database.

Standing at the back door of the house, George pauses to survey the situation. Has he covered all the eventualities? It's a stupid question he knows but he goes through all the possible places where there may be evidence of his presence. He can think of nothing he has not covered so, from the front window facing the street, he makes sure that there is no one in the vicinity of the house. Now, going out of the back door, with his suitcase, he goes to his car parked at the side of the house, backs out carefully and drives away at a moderate speed. There is no way he can guarantee that there are no elderly people residing close by who get their entertainment by watching from behind lace curtains. This is a risk he must take. However, he is as sure as he can be he has not been seen closely enough for identification. Under the circumstances, it is the best he can do.

In a quiet lay-by, at the side of the road, he changes the number plates to a new set and drives on feeling confident that he is safe. Where to go? He feels that he dare not go to his flat in Manchester where he is known as an occasional resident. If a description of him is issued, he might be recognised. He has no doubt. Heading for the M6 motorway, he turns south. East Anglia, with several holiday resorts with Bed and Breakfast lodgings in plentiful supply is just the place to keep his head down and see how things develop in Blackpool. And since it is where George spent much of his childhood, he knows its towns, villages and geography. With fingers firmly crossed for good luck, George drives on south and east to Norfolk.

Chapter 2

Victor Wilson walks through the Elmstone village centre a week before Christmas. It is just after eleven o'clock and the sun is working its way to the south, still casting the longest shadows of the year, and the temperature is nearly as high as it is going to get but still well below freezing. Nonetheless, it is a gorgeous day. There has been a thick frost the previous night and despite the sun, the temperature has not risen sufficiently to melt it. Glistening and sparkling, it reflects and refracts the light into millions of tiny rainbows giving a kaleidoscopic array of colours. The heat, albeit slight, of the sun on his broad shoulders gives Victor an impression of warmth. He is a tall man – classically tall, standing six feet four inches in his socks, dark but short trimmed hair. He is clean shaven with regular, handsome features and weighs over 220 pounds. He is just thirty three years old and is feeling, this winter morning, in top form. He is as fit as he has ever been. His weekly training session the previous night at his rugby club has given him a sense of wellbeing. The loose fitting coat he is wearing covers his flat and muscular stomach but there is no disguising his upper body strength. His biceps fill his sleeves. He and his wife Sarah had made love that morning which itself makes him feel good emotionally and finally, the prospect of an important rugby match on the following day with Christmas day shortly afterwards fill his cup of happiness to the brim. Life could not be better.

Victor is vicar of the parish of Elmstone in rural Suffolk and has been for nearly four years. A bright boy at school, particularly in science, he has been to university where he studied physics. His parents had been keen churchgoers as a result of which he sang in the church choir as choirboy and adolescent. There was a school Scripture Union to which he went with one of his best friends and so it was that Christianity became part of his life just by gradual acceptance – without any Damascus Road conversion or any conscious decision of choice. Almost inevitably at university, he became involved in the Student Christian Movement. It was here that he became close friends with the University chaplain - a forceful individual who, slowly but inexorably, persuaded Victor that he had a calling to the church. The arguments for this were frequently to make choices a question of guilt. "If you ignore your call to the priesthood, you should be ashamed to look Jesus in the face!" He certainly did not have the will power to resist this emotional blackmail. Such pressure was instrumental in making Victor choose the ministry.

However, the Chaplain did encourage Victor to continue with his sport and hence he became very proficient at rugby at which his physique made him an outstanding forward. There is a strange dichotomy about Victor's love of rugby – essentially a violent sport – because Victor is a gentle person with a philosophy of reverence for life based upon one of his adolescent examples – Albert Schweitzer. He would rarely kill anything. Flies, spiders, bees and wasps in the house were trapped under a plastic cup on a window, transported by sliding a cardboard sheet underneath the cup and then released out of doors. The beauty of rugby for him was the opportunity to use his considerable strength and speed in a regulated fashion. In fact, he acknowledges, to get the latent aggression out of his system.

Because of his handsome appearance, Victor was something of a heart throb with the female students and, until he fell under the influence of the Chaplain, had something of a reputation as a womaniser. In fairness to Victor, most of the women that he had relationships with were very willing. It was in his final year that he met Sarah who was then doing post-graduate research in psychology. There was a strong attraction and, before long, they were very much a couple. Victor determined that whatever happened he wanted to spend the rest of his life with this woman. At the same time, he was firming up on his career choice of entering the priesthood and they decided that they would not marry until he had been ordained and Sarah had completed her doctorate in psychology.

Victor has occasional periods of concern about the depths of his beliefs and hence his suitability for his chosen career. He sometimes wonders how he ever managed to get to the situation he is in now, especially given his education in physics and his technical aptitude. The science of physics is all about observing phenomena and then producing hypotheses to explain the observations. If evidence is produced which contradicts the hypothesis then it must be abandoned and a fresh theory put forward which explains the new set of observations. It is also one of the principles of experimental evidence that it must be reproducible or at least observable in the natural world. The problem that troubles Victor is the hypothesis that God created the world and that faith in Jesus combined with repentance for one's sins will lead to everlasting life. It seems that an evidence based philosophy is incompatible with a faith based philosophy.

The problem is that there is no reproducible evidence or any observations supporting the faith that cannot be explained by other theories which are far more likely. The burden on the individual is one of faith. And here Victor faces two issues. In the first place he is not naturally a credulous person. And in the second, even the bible defines faith as "the substance of things hoped for; the evidence of things not seen". In Victor's view, hoping is all very well but hope has never achieved much. Evidence? As far as he can see, there is very little evidence either seen or unseen.

These doubts have often been reinforced by friends and family who have frequently expressed the opinion that he is wasting his life and his talents in the ministry. His father in particular has plainly felt dissatisfied by Victor's choice of career.

"With your abilities and personality, you could do anything and get rich in the process too!"

"But I don't want to do anything else," replies Victor. "And what do riches bring, anyway. Sarah and I are both very happy and in Roy and James we have two great sons. And I know that she enjoys her life and, at least up till now, doesn't appear to miss her work. She's fully occupied with the boys and the parish."

"Well you could certainly have a bigger house and you could use some good holidays in the sunshine somewhere."

"Holidays? But you know that we always go to Sarah's parents in Southwold. It's only just over an hour's drive in our old car. These holidays are always the high point of the children's year. And if they are happy, then so are we. A bigger house? What would we do with that? The Vicarage has four big bedrooms which is quite sufficient for our needs. A bigger car? The one we have always gets us there."

"But it's not your house, is it? And when you retire or leave your job with a tied house you won't have a house. Don't look to me for money. My house will be split four ways between you and your sisters."

"Well, we'll cross that bridge when we come to it," says Victor.

But it is a real point. On his stipend as a priest, he cannot save anything significant and faces the prospect of retiring in 30 or 40 years' time with nowhere to live. Others say to him "God will provide." But evidence for this is not convincing either.

He walks past the Red Lion, a gorgeous 16th century building. It has an enormous arch leading to a courtyard at the rear. The arch was built in the days when top loaded coaches drove through and stopped in the middle to unload passengers' luggage through a trap door overhead. Victor likes the occasional beer there especially on a Monday evening - his day off from his parish duties. Next, he passes the local grocery store of similar age. This has a timbered front with a jetted first floor which this morning is bedecked with a string of fairy lights. He quickly sidesteps a burdened woman clutching two heavy bags of shopping as she leaves the local Co-op grocery store. It is one of his flock, Doris Logan. As she stops, a packet of biscuits topples from the top of one of the bags. Victor sees it coming and is fast enough in his reactions to stoop quickly and catch it just before it hits the ground.

"Morning, Doris," he smiles as he pops it back into the shopping bag and takes it from her as she gropes for her car keys. "Are you well?"

"Morning, Vic, and thank you. Am I well? Well apart from it being Christmas coming up, I'm fine. "

Victor holds up his hands in mock horror. "What heresy is this I'm hearing? Women have been burned at the stake for less. I shall have to report you to the Witchfinder General."

Doris laughs. "It's alright for you," she responds. "You don't have an army descending on you for Christmas day and beyond. Do you think if I prayed enough about it, God would make them stay away?"

"Ah, come off it, Doris," he responds a little sharply. Then he sees that Doris is grinning. Victor's view about divine intervention are well known and are something of a bone of contention in the village. Victor smiles a little wryly.

"All right, all right. I fell for it. Vicars used to be held in respect. I don't know what's happening to the world. Despite that - can I help you with that load?"

"Well, if you wouldn't mind holding these bags while I open the car".

Victor grabs both the bags and lifts them as though they are weightless.

"No problem." And he loads them into the rear of the open car.

"See you soon," he says and sees her drive off.

Doris Logan is one of the church regulars and a real joy to Victor as she has a sense of humour and Victor can be facetious with her – a trait which not everyone appreciates.

The centre of the village is at least four centuries old and he passes a tea shop, a Fish and Chip shop housed in a timbered fifteenth century building and a gift shop of equal antiquity. Then he is clear of the shops and houses and heading past the graveyard within which stands the church. Victor stops to look at it. At the west end, a magnificent steeple towers over the village and the graveyard. At the east is a chancel whose roof line is stepped lower that the rest. The nave of the church is in flint and at the upper level shows a row of clerestory windows separated by decorative flint panels. In the graveyard lie gravestones varying in age from recent years to past centuries. These are decorated at Christmas time with the sparkling frost and in many cases with flowers. If graveyards can ever look welcoming, Victor thinks, this one does. He turns in through the churchyard gate.

As he walks towards the south door drinking in the scene, the last leaf on a beech tree in the graveyard releases its hold on the tree and floats downwards in a death spiral. It lands in front of him and unaware he tramples it flat on to the frosty path. At the same time a cloud passing the sun casts a shadow. To him there is a quite palpable drop in temperature and he gives an involuntary shiver. His mother would have said that someone must have walked over his grave and at the thought he gives a brief smile as he turns the handle of the outer door.

Chapter 3

Sarah traps the ball with her left foot, shimmies to her left sending her eldest son Roy, who is nine years old, to his right then moves quickly past him and then side foots the ball past James who is just over a year younger.

"Goal" she says and punches the air. "Right - I'm going across to the church now. I'll leave you to it. Be careful where you kick that ball. Don't go too close to the gardens or the road." So says Sarah, confident in the knowledge that her words fall on deaf ears. There are none so deaf, she thinks, as boys and men playing with a ball.

Sarah is in her early thirties and is slim and tall although several inches shorter than her husband. Her long dark hair is swept back into a pony tail held with an elastic band. Her nose is too aquiline to be pretty – handsome and full of character would be a better description – and laughter lines are beginning to appear round her full lips. She keeps herself fit in winter by playing with her children and by jogging round the parish footpaths, anything up to five miles a day. In the summer, Sarah also plays tennis at the local club and sometimes cricket as well. There is a thriving ladies' team locally and Sarah can both bat and bowl. Dressed now in somewhat ragged jeans whose holes in the knees are not part of the "designer" trend but simply worn through, topped by a loose T-shirt and a short, bright red jacket, she looks, by clergy wives' standards, a mess. But she moves with real athleticism. It was that slender appearance and fluency of movement which first caused Victor to notice her. That and her total disregard of most dress conventions. This is not an attribute which endears her to some of the older, more rigid members of the congregation such as the Derbyshires. About this, she doesn't care and, to his credit, neither does Victor.

Sarah also knows that she is not approved of by some of the parishioners who regards her as too unconventional - too much of a free spirit. This applies not just to her dress but also to her views on the local Women's Institute and to her children who are, in their view, noisy and undisciplined. Flora Derbyshire, in particular, feels quite free to let her views be known not only to her friends but also to the Vicar.

This frosty morning she is on her way to the church clutching an armful of greenery. Victor will be there already but a token appearance by the vicar's wife is required. Not that Sarah objects to the obligations of the position she holds but she has now been in Elmstone for four years and before that as Victor's wife in a Cambridge parish where Victor was a curate and where their children were born. She does enjoy the position even with its obligations. Thus in the local hairdressers, coffee shop and Co-op she picks up the local gossip and the general feeling of the village on whatever is the issue of the moment.

Sarah's love for Victor had been almost immediate. Physically he was extremely attractive and they had the same interests. She had confidently expected his proposal of marriage, indeed they had discussed the subject several times. She knew, or thought she knew, exactly what marriage to a church vicar would mean, and was prepared to settle for it in the short term. After her doctorate, she had thoroughly enjoyed her career as a university lecturer, but now harbours the desire to return to it as soon as is possible. The downside to the Vicar's wife position, she had discovered, is that it imposes a social barrier, which makes it very difficult to make close female friends – the type with whom she can talk completely openly in the knowledge that it will be totally confidential. Only Kirsten Woodhouse comes into that category and their friendship has been even closer since her husband Bob died over two years before.

There is another aspect to Sarah's personality which is that sometimes, when irritated by the stupidity and ignorance of her husband's parishioners, she can be quite acerbic - not suffering fools as gladly as she perhaps should as vicar's wife.

Victor and Sarah had agreed that she would take no regular employment until the boys were old enough but then she would try to re-engage in her career. One benefit of a tied house which went with the job meant that they are under no financial pressure to buy a house of their own. Given the ratio of house prices as a multiple of salary, at least within one hundred miles of London, there was no way in which they could have bought a house and paid for a mortgage on a priest's salary; even with a university lecturer's pay added they would have been struggling. At the moment, then, they live on Victor's pay. Sarah does a part time job as a teaching assistant in the same local school which the boys attend and such money they bank with a building society, hopefully building up sufficient cash for a deposit. Sarah also stays in touch with her profession by having occasional papers published in the appropriate technical journals. But as she nears ten years away from academic life, she knows that she must return soon or abandon all ideas of resuming her career. What is more, she does want to very much. She misses the intellectual stimulation of the university scene. Although bringing up children through their formative years is, they both feel, a necessity, now aged nine and seven their boys can stand on their own feet a lot more.

Sarah is no deeply convinced Christian, her psychology education having made her too sceptical. Her view on the subject is that thinking man needs a God of some description who is greater than him and requires to be appeased. Thus he invents one. And that has been the story of mankind throughout time and with virtually every race and tribe

Where Victor had his university chaplain as his spiritual guide, Sarah had a similar relationship with one of her lecturers, Bernard Hopper.

"If you feel your future happiness lies with Victor, then marry him and support him. But remember that because he is a scientist his faith is probably fairly fragile."

"It seems strong to me," said Sarah. "He believes firmly in the bible."

"Yes, but just wait until there is some pressure," responded Bernard. "He will be doubting his faith – and with good reason. The bible is regarded in his student circles as the, and Bernard signals quotation marks with two pairs of fingers, "inspired word of God". Irrespective of the fact that it was not finalised as a series of documents until after several hundred years of copying where inevitably mistakes were made and perpetuated either accidentally or deliberately. Such additions have been made as people wanted to put into the mouth of Jesus words that suited their own beliefs. For example, if Jesus didn't actually say "Anything you ask in my name, I will grant it," then they think he ought to have said it and so it was probably added by some scribe. The same applies to Paul's letters – adapted later on to reflect current thinking."

"Are you saying the bible is not reliable?"

"How can it be? It's beyond logic that the writings can be reliable particularly when quoting the actual words spoken – and yet they are persistently thought to be. And I am sure as I can be that at some point Victor will have serious doubts. Victor's beliefs at present are largely emotional but when he applies that considerable intellect logically and scientifically to the situation he'll be struggling. And when that comes he'll need you."

"If he can't trust the bible, what can he believe?"

"What is the over-riding principle of Christianity? It's love, isn't it. Love God. Love thy neighbour. It starts in the Old Testament which is full of it as well. I think the trappings of organised religion and a powerful, hierarchical priesthood are contrary to this main principle. So he has just got to go back to those first principles."

Up until now, as far as she is aware, there have been doubts but there have been no crises. And so, Sarah goes through the motions of the Church of England for her husband's sake but she is more agnostic than believing. More important, at this stage in her career, she is very keen to get back into academic life.

That morning as they were lying awake, gathering the will to get up on a cold morning, Sarah turns towards Victor.

"I've been thinking."

"What - this early?"

Sarah ignores the irony. "I think it's time I started looking for something more in my line than classroom assistant," she remarks. "I'm sure the boys can cope with that and it's not as though you were doing a nine till five job in the City, or anything like that, so we should be able to fit together without depriving them. Frankly, darling, I feel that I have given enough of my life to rearing children and being a wife to the parish. I've got to spread my wings again."

Victor lay thinking about it for a couple minutes. "Yes. I agree. And I confess we've been married for ten years now and the rate at which we are able to save money isn't even keeping pace with inflation. And we don't want to finish in the poor house when we retire."

"Unless you finish up as a bishop."

"Fat chance," says Victor rolling over and nuzzling into his wife's neck. "Or would you find that really sexy?"

"Worth a try," says Sarah putting her arms round his neck and pulling him close.

Chapter 4

The ancient main outer south door of Elmstone church opens into the magnificent vaulted porch. The inner doors from the porch into the church are of the same antiquity and are twelve feet high. These inner doors are usually opened only for weddings and funerals. Its small inset personnel door is normally open but is closed this morning to conserve heat. Like most centuries old churches, this one is a sink for heat because of its height and draughty windows. Through the door Victor can hear the murmur of voices and the faint sound of the organ. He stops to drink in the sounds then lifts the latch that opens the small door and enters, having to stoop low to avoid doing himself serious injury on the five feet high doorway.

Every time he enters the church, Victor glances upwards to the angels. Row upon row they decorate the hammer beam roof. Carved in oak and dating back to the 14th century, there are well over 200 hundred of them, and they seem to Victor to have a presence of their own. In times of stress – of which there are many – he will come and sit quietly alone with them and try to get things into perspective. The church itself has a nave with an aisle on both north and south sides with a chancel at its east end and a bell tower at its west end. The base of the tower is used for the choir to change into their cassocks and surplices before processing up to the chancel where there is a small two-manual organ and two rows of choir stalls on each side. The south door enters about three quarters of the way down the church towards the tower so that late comers can discreetly enter without being too obvious.

Immediately Victor is hit by smells; of greenery, of flowers in profusion and the lingering scent of incense. This visual and scented background is backed by the voices of about a dozen ladies and the organ. There are decorations being placed on each window and, at the rear of the church beside the baptismal font, a single large Christmas tree stands festooned with fairy lights. He recognises that Alan Jones, the organist and Victor's friend is not practising anything in particular but just extemporising on a Christmas carol for his own amusement. But it is a perfect scene, one that brings joy and satisfaction to Victor's heart and removes, at least temporarily, doubts about his calling. This is what Christianity should be all about, he thinks - peace and joy and love.

"Morning, Vicar". Victor turns to the elderly lady who is decorating the window nearest the door. It is Flora Derbyshire who is an indefatigable baker of cakes for the many bring-and-buy sales and other social events which grace the church calendar. Their object is to bring much needed funds into the church coffers but they also foster a community spirit. Her husband, John, now retired, is a churchwarden and is currently clutching a sack of cuttings and other greenery obviously surplus to the requirements of her floral window display. They are a well matched pair - hard workers but over-critical of anything they disagree with and happy to find fault with others. Victor has not had an easy relationship with them as they have objected to some of the new services he has introduced and also the fact that occasionally, for example on the big festivals of the Church, he has used incense during the service. Not only do they object themselves but they spread dissention in the parish. Victor knows that the parish needs them and so for his own peace he tries to appease them and keep them happy. He is aware they have two grown-up children but these are seldom seen. Perhaps, Victor thinks, the parents' critical attitude is unwelcome to their children as it is to him.

"Mrs. Derbyshire. What a gorgeous display! Congratulations to you both!" says Victor, somewhat mendaciously.

Where Doris Logan has a sense of humour and the ridiculous, Flora Derbyshire has no such attribute. She tends to take everything literally and because of that, Victor regrets his remark as soon as it a passed his lips.

"To us both? What has he had to do with it may I ask?" asks Flora sharply – always quick to take offence.

"What a cheek," says John. "I've slaved all morning for a start - although why my wife has to bring at least four times the amount of stuff she actually needs remains a mystery to me every year."

"Oh, Vicar." Flora Derbyshire ignores her husband and drops her voice into confidential mode, "Do you think I should offer to help old Mrs. Dow over there on the middle window? She really isn't up to it and her display lets the whole side down. I could make it a lot nicer."

"Well, perhaps not," says Victor also dropping his voice and knowing, as they both do, that Jane Dow would be mortified. "I think she might be quite upset and in any case it makes your own window look quite outstanding. But it is a very kind offer. Thank you."

"So I've got to take all this lot away with me then, do I?" asks John slightly querulously.

"I'll just remove myself from this marital dispute. Being a referee is not part of the job," says Victor, wishing he had never spoken and with a slightly forced grin. "But congratulations anyway."

"And jubilations," sings out a voice from the other side of the doorway in a fair imitation of Cliff Richard. "HI, Vic!"

Victor turns towards the familiar voice of Kirsten Woodhouse. Kirsten is one of the tragedies that Victor has had to deal with in his ministry in the parish. Bob Woodhouse, a successful architect even at his young age of 35, had been killed in a car accident two years earlier leaving his wife and two young daughters alone. As well as being talented at what he did, Bob was very far sighted and had taken out a substantial insurance policy not only on his own life but also covering his house mortgage. Added to this was the very hefty insurance from the driver whose fault was the cause of Bob's death. The two girls, aged four and six, are with their mother.

"Hello, Jennifer. Hello Margaret," says Victor. "Are you two helping Mummy or are you just getting in the way as usual?"

"We're helping!" they screech simultaneously.

"That's great! Absolutely magic" And then to Kirsten "And how about you? How are things?"

"Struggling along as usual – well, given the time of year, worse than usual, to be honest. But I am moving on, Vic. Slowly but steadily. What else can I do?"

"This will be your third Christmas since Bob died won't it? I do hope it's getting a bit easier. Anyway, I'm glad to see you here. Sarah will be along shortly so you can come back to the Vicarage for a coffee after you're finished. These two young rascals can play with my two hooligans."

Kirsten is a very pretty woman with a kind and loving personality. With shoulder length, fair waved hair and no more than a touch of lipstick and make-up on a flawless complexion she looks like she could join the angels herself. It is the hope of those who know and like her that she will find someone to share her life. With good looks and wealth she should have no difficulty attracting suitors – but Bob will be a hard act to follow.

Victor goes round the church and greets each and every one of the ladies who are decorating the windows and the chancel for Christmas.

As he passes Evelyn Sangster, another of his favourites, he stops and gives a quizzical gaze. She stops what she is doing and straightens up with a red carnation in her hand. "Just putting on the finishing touches," she says.

"Lovely" says Victor. "What is it meant to be?"

Evelyn aims a playful blow at his head. "It's a modern art picture of a rugby player who has just been in a blood bath. And there will be real blood if you don't watch out."

Victor laughs, walks on and stops behind Alan Jones and watches the man at the organ. He never fails to be astonished at the skill of an accomplished organist who can simultaneously handle two or more manual keyboards, a pedal board, a range of stops which can bring various banks of organ pipes into use for each of the keyboards, and a swell pedal to control the volume of one of the manuals. The organist must also read the music and turn the pages while playing and even, from time to time, watch a conductor. It seems superhuman to Victor who is a very modest pianist and who is occasionally required to play hymns in the absence of the organist. This he does on one manual only and with all the stops out. As he watches Alan from behind and above, he notices that the thin area on the crown of Alan's head of dark brown hair is quite a bit larger and thinner than it was four years earlier when Victor first came to the church. Victor guesses that Alan is in his late fifties but despite that there is not a thread of grey to be seen. Victor wonders, not for the first time, if Alan actually dies his hair. Victor looks more closely. Is there a suspicion of fair coloured roots showing? Perhaps Alan is more vain about his appearance than Victor would have guessed.

Alan becomes aware of someone standing behind him.

"And who is that breathing down my neck?" he asks without looking round.

"One guess."

Alan turns. "Haven't you anything better to do than hover over me?"

"No, says Victor. "Should I have?"

"Well, you could be visiting the sick of the parish, for example. That's what you're paid for."

"Is that right?" says Victor with heavy irony. "I never knew. Well, there aren't many sick people in the parish at the moment. And those that are I have seen this morning. So put that into your pipe and smoke it. And I'll be doing sick communions most of Christmas Day as well while you are busy pigging it on turkey and Christmas pudding."

"I wish," says Alan.

"You know perfectly well that you are welcome at our house for dinner in the evening."

"Thanks but no thanks."

The truth is that Alan's private life is a bit of a mystery to Victor despite the four year close acquaintance between the two men. Friendship should be - but is not - the appropriate word for their relationship. Friends should share confidences and be open with each other. However, up to the point when Alan came to the village, which was about the same time as Victor, his previous life is a closed book. When questioned, Alan tends to be reticent about this period. Victor knows Alan's approximate age and that he is retired but on what pension or other income has never been revealed. Perhaps Alan makes his money trading on the Stock Exchange but whatever the source of his funds, all his donations to the church and, as far as Victor is aware, all his payments within the village are done with cash. He lives alone in a large house on the edge of the village and has been married at some time. What has happened to his wife and whether there were any children to the marriage Victor knows not. Alan keeps such secrets locked away and Victor has ceased asking as it has been made very clear by Alan that this area is not to be visited. Whatever his background, Alan is well educated and, because of his ability on the piano and organ has been at some time in a musical environment. And so, being both a competent organist and a generous donor to the church, that is more than enough for Victor to accept him as he is.

There is another connection between Victor and Alan since Alan is a regular spectator at St. Edward's rugby club which plays out of the nearby town of Beckham Market. Victor is one of the star players of their first team, a flank forward who, despite his size, is a formidable weapon in his side's armoury. His speed and strength make him a first choice every week and if it had not been for his vocation he would by now been playing for a bigger club in Cambridge or even for one of the Premier Division clubs.

"So are you fit for tomorrow's game" asks Alan. "And have you a full team?

"Yes on both counts. And we need to be. This will be a real toughie. After our win last year at this game they will be fighting for it. Do you remember that late try I squeezed over?"

"I certainly do – a sheer fluke if I remember correctly. But Victor, It always seems incongruous for someone in your situation to be playing a game which involves such violence. What's happened to "love thy neighbour" for example?"

"But I do love my neighbour. I do like the blokes I play with and against. Join us in the bar afterwards and you will see that usually there is no animosity left over from the game. And it is a game, remember. Played within strict rules controlling the violence"

"Supposed to be," says Alan. "But your opponents tomorrow will be up to every dirty trick in the book that they can get away with. Don't tell me you won't fight back by using the same methods. Violence begets violence."

Victor grins. "Well, we'll do our best to stay within the rules. I presume you'll be there."

"Wouldn't miss it for worlds."

For all his ability to laugh off the violent aspects of rugby, there is a moral issue which concerns Victor. The fact is that he enjoys the physical confrontations which occur – the necessity of hitting the other guy harder than he hits you. And also, when he himself is hurt, especially if it is by foul play away from the sight of the referee, his first inclination is to lash out and really hit the opponent very hard in revenge. Victor knows that he has frequently been a hairsbreadth away from the kind of retaliation which could get him sent off and banned for several weeks from the game. Rugby is a different world where violence is endemic but, in theory, legal violence only. He also knows that such an occurrence would do his future in the ministry no good at all. Not that he has any particular ambition to get advancement to Rural Dean or even Dean or Bishop, but it is occasionally there in his mind as a long term future possibility.

Victor looks round and sees that his wife has entered the church at the back. As he looks down the church towards her, she simultaneously meets his eye and gives a quick grin of acknowledgement. He gives Alan an affectionate tap on the shoulder and strolls down to meet her. Sarah's presence makes a difference to Victor. She is so much part of him, that he has a strange feeling of incompleteness when she is not with him and when she joins him, wherever that may be, it always feels like a slight lifting of load from his shoulders.

Victor comes up and gives Sarah a kiss on the cheek. "Where are our two ruffians?"

"On the playing field over the road kicking a ball about. I've brought a pile of greenery to see if anyone needs any more. Kirsten says she could use a couple of sprays of eucalyptus in her arrangement."

"Have you asked her round for coffee afterwards?"

"Yes, she has," interrupts Kirsten, "but I've got to get into town for some shopping, so I really have to get going now."

"That's a shame," says Victor. "Sarah, when are we going across to Southwold?"

"Not till the Sunday after Christmas. If you do that Sunday morning service, then we can be off. After the Midnight Mass, then three Christmas day services, plus half a dozen home communions, you are going to be absolutely whacked. And that will suit Mum and Dad very well too. Kirsten, I'm sorry you can't come along. There just isn't enough room in the Wilson house."

"Don't even think about it" says Kirsten. "I'm going away to see my parents in Sheringham on Boxing Day. They're really very keen to see their grandchildren and no doubt Father Christmas will visit there as well as here."

Alan is walking down the centre aisle of the church and passes by.

"How are things, Kirsten?" he asks. "Going away over Christmas?"

"Everything's fine" says Kirsten. "And yes, we're going away on Boxing Day for a few days."

"I'll maybe see you before that. If I don't, I hope you have a good time."

"Same to you."

Victor walks homewards with Sarah and the children. Hand in hand they cross the road towards the playing field where their two boys are playing happily on the playground equipment. Despite her ambitions to resume her career as soon as possible, Sarah appears to be happy in her life and Victor is basking in it. He feels that his cup of happiness is full to overflowing and offers a silent thanks to his God. Could life get any better? Not without a certain feeling of self-satisfaction he thinks that it probably cannot. He does not pursue the logic of that thought to reflect that, in this situation, things can only get worse.

"Dad, Dad." Shouts greet them as they walk across the field. "Dad, can we play rugby?"

"After lunch" says Sarah "if your father can spare the time."

"Just about," says Victor, grinning. He runs towards them collects the football and proceeds to dribble around teasing them to take the ball from him. Finally, laughing together they set off for home.

Chapter 5

George is not is a good mood. The bed and breakfast house he is staying in is small, but his room is reasonably spacious. It is probably the best room in the house but that is because it is just before Christmas and the holiday trade in north Norfolk is non-existent. The outlook from the window is depressing as the house is set in a street of terraced houses. It has a carpeted entrance lobby with a hall table and a bentwood hatstand containing, more for decoration than utility, a number of walking sticks and umbrellas. Stairs rise to the first floor where there are three bedrooms, each en-suite with a toilet and shower room. In each case this has been partitioned off the bedroom itself and so is tiny. The room itself has a double bed, a chest of drawers with a toilet mirror perched on it, a small television set located almost at ceiling level in one corner of the room, an easy chair and a wooden dining chair next to the drawers. The breakfast, in this establishment is in quantities measured to the last cornflake and bacon sliced so thin that, if dropped, it would float to the ground like a sheet of tissue paper. George had chosen it because it was in a street of nondescript terraced houses.

"Lovely breakfast," says George each morning with an irony which is lost on his landlady.

She, a buxom widow of uncertain years, acts as though she is mistress of the Ritz. But the place and its accommodation is the least of his worries. His major problem is that he is possibly on the run from the police. He has seen nothing in the press or TV news but that is no guarantee of safety.

George is now on the other side of the country from Blackpool and in the small seaside town of Sheringham on the Norfolk coast. It is a town and an area which he knows reasonably well having been brought up in the town of Ipswich in Suffolk. He sits in his bedroom not totally out of ready cash but reluctant to broach any of his bank accounts. He wonders what to do. The sad fact is that he is without contacts or friends whom he can sponge off – except… except, he thinks, possibly his father. His relationship there is non-existent. George now wonders whether it is worth the cost of a phone call to get the almost inevitable rejection. But it is Christmas Day in a couple of days' time and to stay where he is will itself be suspicious - so perhaps there is nothing to lose. He decides that he will telephone his father that evening when, if his routine is as usual, he should be at home.

To pass the time, George switches on his miniscule TV set. The placement of the screen means that the only way George, or anyone else, can watch it in any kind of comfort is by lying on his bed. He is just in time for the early evening news.

"And the headlines to-night" says the newsreader, a tall attractive woman in her forties who betrays her education by standing with her feet in a ballet position. George is so busy admiring her shapely legs that he is barely aware of what she is saying.

"The body of a woman has been found in a house in Blackpool. The death appears to have been accidental but the police wish to interview a man who had been staying with her. The person concerned is requested to report to the police in Blackpool."

It is just as well that George is lying down as he would have fallen off a chair had he been sitting. Suddenly he is giving the television his maximum attention. The details which follow leave him in no doubt. Although the name is not mentioned the body involved must be that of Cynthia. What worries him most is that Cynthia may have been talking to someone else. And if so, what did she say about George? If the person who had reported George's existence had been in some way intimate with Cynthia then Cynthia's suspicions about George's position and motives might also have been communicated to the friend and thus to the police. Alternatively, George's reported presence may simply have been the work of one of the neighbours observing the scene from behind net curtains. At least that, from George's point of view, would be less dangerous although, on the other hand, he might have been seen and therefore could be described.

Either way, it is high time that George moves somewhere he can have a very low profile. And so it is time he phoned home. The phone is answered by his father.

George's relationship with his father is not a happy one. From the age of twelve, during his formative years, it had been getting worse year on year. His father is convinced, with good reason but without recognising that his own lack of parental attention and care has been contributory, that his son is a bad lot. His involvement with a street gang involved in organised shop lifting and his expulsion from school for cheating at exams came as no surprise. His sacking from his first, and only job, for theft of the petty cash has left his parent with a disgust for his only son. This disgust is largely because of George's stupidity in committing crimes where he is easily identified and caught. George's only regret at the time seemed to be that he was unlucky to be caught. As to his attitude for cheating and thieving, the way he saw it is that the systems in place simply encourage dishonesty.

"They're just asking for it," was George's attitude. "If they leave the petty cash tin open on the desk, what do they expect? As for cheating at exams, if I can take in information with me and answer the question that way – isn't that passing the paper by being smart rather than memorising the facts. And anyway, is your own background totally honest?"

George's father feels there is no point in even trying to answer to that. After all, he thinks, whose background is totally honest? The last time they met his parting words had been "George, I never want to see you again."

And so, two days before Christmas George phones.

"Hi, Dad. How are you doing?"

There is a long pause and a deep sigh from the other end of the line.

"George, have you forgotten the last thing I said to you? I never want to see you again and that means talk to you as well."

"Oh, Dad. Can't you let bygones be bygones? Of course I haven't forgotten you or what you said but I just thought that with Christmas here it was time to make a fresh start with the pair of us. Can't I just come and stay with you for two or three days over Christmas?"

"George. You just don't get the message do you? My friends here don't even know of your existence and there's no way you're going to come here out of the blue and making me explain that I've disowned you and kept you out of my life. I'm not going to do it."

"Dad, suppose I just come and keep a low profile – stay in the house and keep out of everyone's way. I just want to see you again and show you how I' m getting on. I'm doing O.K. now."

"But you don't even know where I live."

George gives a little laugh. "Do me a favour, Dad," he says. "Yes, I do. That's how I know your number. You haven't been following me but I've been following you. I often come through your village and past your house. I saw you once but didn't dare to stop as I didn't want to upset you. I have even enquired about you in the local shops. Of course, they know nothing about you or your past and I've no intention of telling anybody. But I would like to make amends for the grief I gave you and show you that I'm on the straight and narrow."

There is another long pause.

"All right, George. Where do you live now?"

"Normally I live in Manchester but I'm quite close at the moment actually. I'm here on business and I have to be back here after Christmas so I could be with you in a couple of hours."

"Look, I'll leave my car on the drive. Just drive straight into the garage and close the doors."

This suits George's requirements exactly.

"O.K. Dad. That'll be fine. I'll see you in about a couple of hours. Thanks, Dad."

George smiles to himself. He is confident that he will be able to spend some time at home. He can plead business visits in the East Anglian area which make it important to stay for a couple of weeks. This should give him time to allow things to quieten down.

Chapter 6

The big day has arrived and Victor gets up from bed where he has had an early night and a lie-in to preserve his stamina for the afternoon rugby match. The coming contest occupies his thoughts almost entirely and he is uncharacteristically quiet during breakfast. Breakfast is taken in the kitchen which, with a large gas-fired stove-and-oven unit, is the warmest place in the house. For extra hydrocarbon intake he treats himself to four slices of thick toast smothered in butter and marmalade and a large plate of porridge. The family usually do not sit around the kitchen table on a Saturday morning and this morning is no exception. Both boys are still in their beds and Victor and Sarah are alone.

"Hello, hello. Are you in there somewhere?" Sarah knocks sharply on the deal table in their large kitchen.

"What, what?" stammers Victor. "Did you say something?"

"Only three times" says Sarah. "Where were you?"

"Sorry, darling. I was just making a break on the blind side of the scrum and heading towards the try line. What did you say?"

"Have you forgotten that you are taking a wedding at one o'clock?"

"Ah, yes" says Victor who has forgotten entirely. "But that shouldn't be a problem. If the bride is on time we should be through by half past one which gives me plenty of time to get home, pick up my kit and get to the ground by two o'clock for a 2.30 kick off."

"Two fifteen isn't it, this time of the year?"

Victor does not generally swear but the shock of this remark is too much.

"Sugar!" he expostulates. "Is it?" And after a short pause. "Well, it should still be OK. I just won't be able to hang around with the wedding party afterwards."

"Dear, oh dear. What would you do without me? Let's hope the bride is on time."

"Well, I'm sure I made it clear that I wouldn't tolerate any traditional 'bride must arrive late' nonsense."

"Let's hope your words sank in."

At one o'clock, Victor is standing at the church door with no sign of any bridal car. The bridegroom is there, the best man and even the bridesmaids have arrived in their own conveyance. Victor goes over to them.

"She was ready quarter of an hour ago. I can't understand it" says the mother of the bridesmaids.

Just then one of the congregation comes up to Victor.

"I'm sorry, Vicar" he mumbles "but I've just had a call on my mobile. The bride's car has broken down and they are having to get another. They'll be about fifteen minutes before they are here."

Victor groans, then has an idea. He goes to the church gate where there is the usual collection of villagers who come to every wedding to look and comment about what the bride is wearing. He spots a young girl of about fifteen whom he knows.

"Gwennie. Please will you do me a big favour." Gwennie nods.

"Nip across to the vicarage and ask Sarah for my rugby kit. It's all packed but I need it here now."

Gwennie dashes off and Victor continues to chew his nails in anxiety. The time scale is getting tighter and tighter. In five minutes she is back and there is still no sign of the bride. Victor grabs the kit bag and nips through to the vestry. Quicker than he has ever changed before, he strips off his cassock and surplice, shirt, trousers and socks and dresses himself in his rugby kit including his rugby boots. He then re-dons his priestly kit and gets back to the church door just as the car rolls up with the bride and her father. Fortunately his boots have got rubber cleats to give good grip on the turf so are quiet on the church tiled floor and, apart from having a go-faster white stripe along them, are not particularly noticeable. Luckily also his cassock not only brushes the floor but buttons up to the throat so his lack of a clerical dog-collar cannot be seen. So, despite his heart now going at over one hundred beats a minute, he is able to present an unruffled appearance and, in any case, all eyes are on the bride. The bride's father apologises which Victor brushes off as being unnecessary in the circumstances and the little group proceeds up the nave to the chancel screen with Victor leading the way a touch more briskly than the normal stately pace for such events.

Through all this Alan Johnson has been manfully playing the organ and getting nearly as agitated as Victor.

Now Victor recognises that the day is the biggest in the lives of the young couple and thus he restrains himself with great difficulty from rushing through the service as fast as he can. And so the service goes ahead, the wedding pair exchange their vows, the organ plays and the choir sings. Only at the signing of the register does Victor hurry things along as, given the chance, the couple would spend all afternoon taking photographs. And then the service is over, the wedding procession goes down the church and out of the main door now wide open despite the cold weather and pursued by a shortened version of the Widor Toccata on the organ. Alan obviously has the same destination in mind.

Victor declines the invitation to be photographed along with the wedding party citing a previous engagement for which he is already late. No one seems unduly disappointed at this and Victor is free to walk as quickly as possible back to the vestry. He grabs his kit bag with his normal day clothes and dashes from the side chancel door to his car. The wedding guests look on in some bemusement as the vicar who has just conducted the ceremony with great solemnity is seen racing across the churchyard to his car with his cassock hitched above his knees and his surplice flying in the wind behind him.

As he drives, he glances at his watch and is appalled to see that he will arrive just as the players are going out onto the pitch. And indeed, despite driving like a Formula One racing driver, heart in mouth, such is the case. His travel time is not helped by the fact that the entry to the rugby ground is on a bit of dual carriageway and to get to it, it is essential to go to the roundabout a hundred yards further, go round it and turn in to the ground on the return leg. A queue at the roundabout is no help to his timing or to his temper. He drives into the ground at high speed and, unable to find a free parking spot, stops his car in the middle of the carpark. He leaps out and races towards the pavilion as fast as his cassock will allow. The whole scene is now visible from the pavilion. This has a bank of seating in front and a balcony at first floor level which is packed with spectators. The players are now leaving the pavilion and going onto the pitch but all attention is on the flying cassock and when the figure within is recognised a loud but ironic cheer breaks out.

The coach, Chris Cooke, is standing just outside the pavilion doors holding them open for Victor.

He shouts to an assistant, "Jerry, get Jeff Black off the field. Now!"

He follows Victor into the changing room and stands over him fuming. "Christ Almighty! Where the fuck have you been. Our biggest game of the season and you can't be arsed to arrive in time. I'm fucking pissed off with you."

Now, normally, no one in the club uses bad language particularly religious oaths when Victor is within earshot. It's a friendly club and no one likes to cause offence to anyone, particularly Victor. His club mates know that Victor cannot treat such vulgarity lightly – what he calls "taking the Lord's name in vain". Victor takes it personally as a hurt and as an insult to his profession. His normal reaction is to show sadness and disappointment but this time Victor, being entirely in the wrong, takes it in silence as he divests his clerical garb as quickly as possible.

Victor rushes out to the pitch to ironic cheers from several hundred supporters in the small stand. The referee just stops himself blowing for the start, Victor takes up position and poor Jeff Black has to walk ignominiously off the field.

It is a universal truth that any sportsman or woman about to take part in an important game or match needs to have time to concentrate upon the matter in hand and to eliminate any external influences. This simple lesson is the first of two Victor learned from the day's events and which would affect his play. While at the back of an early scrum, Victor is concentrating on pushing as best he can - but also thinking of what had just happened. Would Jeff Black ever forgive him? Was he too abrupt in refusing to take part in any photographs after the wedding and did he cause offence? With this train of thought circulating in his brain he is not ready for the opposing scrum-half making a break down his side of the scrum. Too late in seeing it he is left looking a complete idiot as he clutches at thin air. The scrum-half takes the ball up to the full-back, draws him into a tackle and slips a well-timed pass to his own flank forward for an easy try underneath the posts. A simple conversion follows with the result; 7-0 for the opposition!

Victor is humiliated. No one in his side looks him in the eye. They don't need to. Everyone on both sides and in the crowd knows exactly who is at fault.

The second sporting lesson is more personal. It is important in a violent game like rugby not to lose one's temper whatever the provocation. Thus, later in the first half, St. Edwards has clawed back to a three point advantage. Victor, now playing with some conviction and determined to make up for his earlier error has tackled the opposition scrum half. The pair are immediately enveloped by a collection of forwards from both sides so that Victor and his opponent are at the bottom of the ruck. Suddenly Victor experiences extreme agony in his groin. This is caused by someone gripping his testicles and squeezing hard. Victor finds it hard not to scream out loud but the whistle blows and the players pull themselves off the pile of bodies. Last to get up are Victor and the malefactor who turns out to be his opposite number flank forward. This individual makes a play of smelling his hand and then wiping it on his shorts, all the while grinning while he does so. Victor is seething with anger and is sorely tempted to punch him in the face. However, he restrains himself with difficulty. "You bastard" he mutters.

However, retribution is not long delayed. The next time the flanker comes round the scrum Victor tackles him round the waist, picks him up and spikes him. This is, in modern times, an illegal action involving as it does in the tackle, not bringing the player straight to the ground but picking him up, turning him over and dropping him onto his head. This is a practice totally outlawed since it can lead to severe damage to the spine. Victor is heedless of this and of the consequences. The consequences are not long in coming. When it has been established that the player has sustained no real damage, the referee whips out his red card and Victor has to make the long, shameful walk to the changing rooms.

"Victor, what the hell are you playing at to-day?" The club coach has followed Victor inside and is furious. "First you arrive late and now you have probably lost us the game. If you want to play first team rugby you've got to give it first priority."

"I do, I do" mumbles Victor. "It wasn't my fault – the bride was late and then the bastard grabbed my balls."

"The bride's always late," says the coach. "You bloody well know that and it's your responsibility to organise your time better or give up the game. I suggest you had better get out of here before half time as there won't be any sympathy."

And so Victor is left nursing a bruised body and spirit. At home, sitting on the sofa he gets Job's comfort from his ever loving wife but little in sympathy. In fact she, with all the wisdom of the afterthought, rubs salt into the wound.

"Never mind, dear" says Sarah. "It's only a game. I love you dearly but you really must control that temper. This won't do you any good at all, you know. I wouldn't be surprised if the Bishop were to have something to say on the subject. You're not only letting yourself down, you're letting the whole Church down."

Victor knows that Sarah knows that this type of patronising is extremely irritating to him and being a psychologist she knows exactly how to turn the screw to show how fed up she is with his performance.

Victor can only grit his teeth and bury his head in his hands. Sarah sits beside him and gives him a hug. Victor groans in misery.

Chapter 7

Christmas Eve. The night is dark and starless due to total cloud cover. The threat of imminent snow is strong – palpable due to the slight rise in temperature which often precedes a snowfall. People from all over the village are heading to the church. Even the local pubs empty and the drinkers make their way, some homeward and some churchward. Cries of "Happy Christmas" ring out. Inebriation is no barrier to following tradition and turning up at the midnight service.

George is arriving deliberately late to the Christmas Eve midnight service so as to reduce the number of people who will see him - including his father who left at least half an hour ahead of him. He enters the church just as the choir are processing from the rear of the church where they have, in the area at the base of the bell tower, changed into their blue cassocks and white surplices. At the rear of the procession comes the person whom George supposes to be the vicar of the parish. George's entry coincides with the vicar's passing the cross aisle that leads from the south door to the north door and inevitably the priest's attention is captured by the movement. George sees the vicar glance briefly in his direction. It is only a glance and so short that George thinks that there is no way that the vicar will have seen enough to recognise him. He hopes so, anyway, and finds himself a seat at the very rear of the nave partly concealed by a pillar. This seat is vacant because from this position anyone is obscured from the choir stalls including the vicar's stall which is behind the chancel screen. However, from this position George is able to scan most of the congregation at his leisure. The church is packed right to the very rear.

George's motives in attending the service are not in any way religious despite being forced to attend church as a child. His presence this evening is simply to get out of the house where he has been effectively imprisoned for the previous two days and, more importantly, to scan the field for suitable talent for his next conquest. He is well aware that his father will act as an impediment to his forming any relationship within the village but, if the opportunity should arise, George is confident that he will find a way to overcome that.

The hymns and readings awaken forgotten memories for George and he finds himself shaking his head in amazement that people can be so gullible to believe such rubbish and when it comes to the sermon he is in a totally sceptical frame of mind. The vicar maintains that selfishness is the driving force for individuals and societies today. He tries to impress his congregation with the philosophy that the solution for the individual and for society as a whole is for the "haves" to see where they can give and for those who only take from society to look for where they can give something in return. This is at odds with George's own philosophy which is that life is a jungle and that you survive by taking what you can and to hell with the rest. To hell with himself also if that is the end result of his own philosophy.

The slight problem that George has at that moment is that there is no way for him to hide from the man in the pulpit and he is aware that even as the Vicar is speaking his eyes are roaming the congregation presumably making a mental note of who is there. George keeps his head down so that he cannot make eye contact again so does not notice that the vicar's eyes stay on him for a second or two.

As the worshippers return from the altar having taken communion, George is positioning himself to see the individuals properly. Not surprisingly there are several apparently unattached females who fall into the category of age and quality to attract him.

At the end of the service, George is slow to anticipate what is going to happen and is caught by surprise as the vicar goes straight to the church door instead of following the choir into the base of the bell tower. So instead of making an early exit he decides to delay and hope to get out in the crush of the rest of the congregation. Although a large proportion of the people stand around wishing each other "Happy Christmas" there comes a point where a few who are probably once a year attenders at best, aim to get past the vicar as he is talking to a young woman at rather more length. As he is passing with head turned away from the Vicar he overhears:

"Well, have a good holiday in Sheringham, Kirsten, and give my regards to your parents."

What a coincidence! George is intrigued. There is no evidence of a man in attendance so perhaps the woman is unattached for some reason. While most of the congregation are milling around outside the church door, he waits in the darkness outside the church gate for the woman to leave. She eventually comes and heads off in the direction of an estate of large new houses built on the edge of the village. In so doing she passes George.

"What a lovely service," says George.

The lady pauses momentarily. "Yes, wasn't it?" she responds as she moves away.

"And it's going to snow, I think" adds George.

"I hope so," says the woman over her shoulder.

"Happy Christmas".

The woman does not respond as she walks away into the silent darkness but George has made contact and wonders how he can renew the acquaintance. He heads in the opposite direction towards his father's house and into deeper darkness. He wants to get there well before his father who, he knows, will be one of the last to leave the church.

At the house, George, having made sure that there is no evidence that he has been out, waits for his father's return.

"How was the service?" he enquires.

"Fine."

"Many there?"

"Yes."

"I thought of coming but decided you would think me hypocritical."

"You can do what you like."

George flares up. "You're never going to give me the benefit of the doubt are you, Dad. You've just made up your mind that I am bad one and that's an end to it. And it's not as if your own past was snow white pure. Well, have a happy Christmas."

His father replies in sorrow. "You forget, George, that I've known you for your whole life. I know what you're like and, yes, I know you're a bad one. And any crimes I may have committed are worlds away from your ones. Now let's go to bed and I'll see you in the morning."

"Can't we just have a little whisky together for Christmas sake?"

George's father stops and sighs.

"All right, George. Just because it's Christmas."

"And I promise I'll leave on Boxing Day."

"Very well."

Kirsten meanwhile heads quickly for home to relieve the baby-sitter. She pays over the agreed fee of twenty pounds fee and another twenty on top.

"Oh, Mrs Woodhouse, there's no need for that. I'm happy to baby-sit for you any time."

"Take it as a Christmas present. I don't know what I would do without you."

Alone, Kirsten sits down and weeps in her misery. It is the worst time for her. Birthdays and anniversaries are also bad but Christmas always seemed to be a special time of love between her and her husband. The loneliness is heart breaking and Kirsten cannot resist the thought that perhaps she should look for someone now to fill the gap in her life. But life must go on and Kirsten heads upstairs to do initial packing in preparation for her visit to Sheringham.

She does get on well with her parents and since they adore the girls it should be a pleasant week with them.

Victor arrives at home. Every one after the midnight service is anxious to get back to their families and Victor is no exception. He walks through the empty streets, enjoying the peace and the silence. Sarah is waiting for him inside the door and they hug each other for several minutes.

"You know, my love, being with you all my worries and troubles simply disappear. It's amazing."

"I do know and it's the same for me."

Eventually, Sarah asks "How about a small whisky to relax you even further?"

"I don't really need it," says Victor "but since you ask let's have one. It'll make me sleep better and remember, I've still got a busy day ahead tomorrow."

"You mean today."

Victor groans. As they each sip a small whisky, Sarah asks

"How was the service? Usual suspects turned up?"

"Yes, and a few extra as usual - mostly villagers who turn up once a year and at weddings or funerals."

"Well, I'd rather have them in than out. At least you can talk to them if they're in front of you."

"I suppose you're right. Actually, there was one stranger – a fellow I didn't recognise and who kept himself at a distance. As I was saying my farewells at the door, he sneaked past without me having the chance to talk to him. I presume he's staying in the village but he didn't seem to be with anyone else. Very odd."

"Would you know him again?"

"Oh, yes. And if I see him, I'll have a word with him. I wouldn't like any one to think that we're unfriendly."

"Perhaps he'll come to one of the services tomorrow."

"Perhaps. Anyway, let's to bed - as the bard says. I feel something coming on."

"My first Christmas present?"

"You never know your luck."

Later, they are lying in bed together in perfect contentment, tired and warm after a long day and a hot bath. Victor has got into bed without his normal pyjamas. He reaches across to Sarah and finds, to his satisfaction, that she also is naked. Their lovemaking is slow and tender and before long Victor rolls across on top and finds his insertion smooth and easy. In that embrace they remain until Victor feels Sarah beginning to move underneath him. He then starts to move in sympathy and, to their common satisfaction and joy, they climax together.

Victor raises his head and looks at his wife. She is slightly flushed but smiling and, with her hair spread across the white pillow, she has never looked lovelier. He drops a kiss on her forehead.

"Happy Christmas," he whispers.

Sarah's smile broadens. "So far, so good," she says.

Chapter 8

Sheringham – the Norfolk seaside town famous as a holiday resort and a championship golf course. This spectacular terrain runs along the top of coastal cliffs overlooking the North sea. These sheer cliffs tower from 100 to 200 feet above a shingle beach. When the tide is out, however, a smooth sand beach is revealed. The course is bounded on the inland side by another major attraction of the area which is a steam train, privately owned and run by volunteers. This goes from Sheringham to Holt which is some 15 miles to the west The town goes back many centuries, the older parts now being on the east side. At the foot of the High Street there is the oldest part where short narrow, twisting streets create a one way traffic system.

There are many hotels in the resort, one a large imposing building in red brick on the front but many others, mostly in the west part of the town. Additionally, there are a large number of bed and breakfast establishments scattered around the town. It is in one of those where George stayed when he first came to the town and having retained his room there for a modest charge, it is to where he returns from his father's house on Boxing Day. With an idea forming in his mind about how to get to know Kirsten, he walks to the town centre past several hotels and makes a note of one which is both open and which looks reasonably high class.

The shopping area of Sheringham is quite limited and George reckons that it is a fair bet that Kirsten will, sooner or later – preferably sooner – walk along the main street. There he finds a small café close to the clock tower which marks the centre of the town. He sits near the

43

window from where he can see all the passing traffic and pedestrians. At this time of the year, holiday makers are in short supply and spotting Kirsten should not be difficult. At any rate, he has nothing better to do and it is worth spending some time on the project.

Sure enough, after half an hour of waiting he spots her walking slowly along the street and window shopping as she goes. George quickly pays his bill, leaves the coffee shop and hurries down the opposite side of the street where Kirsten is strolling, then turns, crosses over the street and walks towards her. He times his meeting to coincide with Kirsten as she is leaving one window and heading to the next and "accidentally" bumps into her.

"Sorry," says George.

"Sorry, my fault. I wasn't looking," says Kirsten.

"Good heavens. Aren't you from Elmstone? Didn't we meet just outside the church?"

Kirsten looks a bit mystified.

"Just after the midnight service on Christmas Eve – I mean, Christmas Day" prompts George.

"Oh, yes" Kirsten remembers. "Golly, it was so dark I'm surprised you recognised me"

"To be honest, I noticed you inside the church and I never forget a beautiful woman," George knows this faux gallant approach is risky as it turns off his target as often as it turns her on. However, he has sized up Kirsten accurately which, since she is extremely pretty and no doubt has been told so many times, is not surprising.

Kirsten laughs. "Apart from that – what are you doing here?"

"Well, I was here before Christmas on business and I've still got some more to do."

"You're doing work between Christmas and New Year?" she asks in some disbelief.

"No. But I live alone in Manchester and I thought I might as well spend the holiday week here on my own rather than in my flat. But while we're at it, what are you doing here. You live in Elmstone don't you? But rather than chat here in the cold, why don't we have a cup of coffee over there. It looks quite pleasant."

Kirsten is not quite sure how to handle this but George seems fairly personable and she agrees and lets him lead her into a nearby café.

At this point in his foreplay, George is at his best. Teasing, laughing, but not too boisterously, always interested in the subject of his attentions he is quickly forming a friendship with Kirsten. Before long, Kirsten has apprised George of her entire history including, and, if not full details of her financial positon, at least sufficient to give a George a fair idea of her affairs. She is an independently wealthy, single mother holidaying with her parents for a week with her two daughters. Apart from the parents and the two daughters, it couldn't be better, thinks George.

"So here I am, George," she says sadly. "Having a coffee with a friend is the nearest I get to having a good time."

George places his hand over hers. "You've had it tough," he commiserates. "Maybe next year will bring something new into your life."

Kirsten leaves her hand where it is.

As they are drinking their coffees, George, for his part, is filling out his own position. He skates through his personal history but omits any mention of his parents and sketches out his business career, for the most part imaginary. He has also hinted at the brilliant ideas he has for developing the business frustrated only by lack of finance and the short sightedness of the banks.

"Don't get the impression I'm on my uppers, Kirsten," he says. "I mean I'm doing alright but it could be so much better. The banks have no idea about business opportunities and always want cast iron security for any loans."

George claims that his reason for being in the village at the midnight service was because he had once many years ago been in Elmstone and been enchanted by the church – not least its collection of angels.

"The place is so atmospheric – I really feel at peace," says he, soulfully.

"Yes," agrees Kirsten. "I feel exactly the same."

"I must say, Kirsten, meeting you has been really fortuitous. I've enjoyed this chat enormously. Do you think you could bear to have dinner with me sometime? I'm staying at the Grand."

"I'd love to."

"This evening? At my hotel?"

"Yes. I'm sure that'll be fine. I'll just tell my Dad and Mum that I've met an old friend and I'm sure they will be happy."

"An old friend? I'm flattered," says George.

"It certainly feels like you're an old friend, George."

"Shall I pick you up?"

"Perhaps not. My parents might not be so happy if they see a tall handsome man so I'll let them think it is a girlfriend."

"Whatever you prefer," says George thinking as he does so that things could not possibly be going better. Even if there is little chance of a long term relationship, at least he should be able to get her into his bed if not the first night at least before she has to go back home at the end of the week. So he says "au revoir" to Kirsten and seals it with a cheek to cheek chaste kiss which Kirsten makes no effort to resist. She heads towards the seafront where there are several blocks of apartments. George follows her at a discreet distance until he sees her enter one which he assumes belongs to her parents.

He heads off to the chosen hotel where he feels certain that he will be anonymous. There he books and pays for a double room for the night and a table for two for dinner that evening.

Paying for things like hotels is always tricky for George, or anyone else who does not want to leave evidence of his passing. The need to avoid a trail of credit card or even card payments is essential. George tends to use cash wherever possible. He picks up the cash from ATMs but never in the place where he is staying – always in a town or, preferably, a service station he is passing. At present, his wallet is stuffed with five hundred pounds, picked up earlier, which he knows would be enough to cope with his B and B bill and other expenses.

He goes back to the boarding house and picks up his small travelling suitcase and some night attire and shaving kit. He sticks his head round the door to the private room where his landlady is watching television.

"I'm going out for the evening," he announces, "and won't be back till late. So please don't stay up for me. I'll let myself in and I'll be very quiet so as not to wake you."

"Have a good evening."

"Thanks."

George goes first to the hotel where he registers using a fictitious name, settles into his room and then waits in the lobby of the hotel at half past seven as they had agreed.

Kirsten is wearing a warm coat which is cut to perfection. When George takes it from her, she reveals a dark grey low-cut dress which goes just to knee level.

"Wow," he says with real conviction, "You look absolutely gorgeous."

Kirsten dimpled and lowered her eyes in false modesty. "Thank you, kind sir," she responded quoting from the nursery rhyme.

"And is your face your fortune?" asks George, dredging the childhood poem from the depths of his memory.

Kirsten giggles charmingly. "Fortunately I don't have to rely on that."

"You're too modest. Why don't you come up to my room and we'll leave your coat there? I have a table booked in quarter of an hour – not that there is any rush. The place is half empty."

There is an atmosphere of excitement between them. Both of them know what might happen later on. In George's case it is what he is planning and in Kirsten's case she thinks it is what George is planning. She is at least half hoping that events will proceed in that direction. It is over two years since Bob has died and she has had no sexual experience. The thought that to-night might be the night for breaking the drought is making her quite breathless with the tension of anticipation. That tension communicates itself to George.

In the room, he opens the mini bar and opens a half bottle of red wine from the room bar. "Just a little snifter to get us in the mood?" he suggests.

"Yes, please."

"Your good health, Kirsten. And thanks for making my day."

"Likewise."

Kirsten is too nervous to sit down and she tours the room looking at the pictures that are hung on the walls. She picks up the TV remote control and switches on. It is yet another cooking programme. George watches her in some amusement. This is all working splendidly. Eventually, they finish their drinks and go down to dinner. As they leave the room, George takes the plastic card key out of the power switch, the lights and the television go off and they leave the room and head for the lifts to the ground floor.

Dinner goes as well as either of them could have expected. The service is excellent, the room is warm George orders a bottle of New Zealand Sauvignon Blanc with the fish and with their fillet steaks an excellent and expensive Crozes-Hermitage. By this time it is nearly ten o'clock and they have been enjoying each other's company for over two and a half hours. Given the wine in George's room and the two bottles with the meal, Kirsten has drunk the best part of a full bottle of wine and is more than a little tipsy.

"Shall we have coffee in my room?" suggests George.

Kirsten is a little coy. "Why not?" she asks. There must be several reasons why not but she can't think of any at that very moment.

And so, slowly, they make their way to the lifts. One is waiting and once inside, Kirsten leans against George and raises her face to be kissed. George obliges and they only break off when the lift doors open. With Kirsten hanging on him, George fishes out his key, opens the door and pops the key into the electrical slot. Kirsten sits heavily on the bed but as she does so, the television bursts into life. It is the Ten O'clock news.

"Police are circulating the identikit picture of a man they wish to interview in connection with the death in Blackpool of Cynthia Reynolds."

There is a picture of a man which, as far as identikit drawings go, is quite a reasonable depiction of George. Both George and Kirsten look at the screen. George grabs the remote from where Kirsten has left it and switches the television off. In so doing he is both too quick and too slow. Too slow in anticipating what is coming but also too quick in reacting and switching off. Their eyes meet. Kirsten's look turns from one of questioning to one of shock and George instantly knows that Kirsten has guessed the worst.

"These pictures are useless," gasps George in an attempt to brush the situation aside.

Kirsten looks at him in something approaching horror.

"That's you, George, isn't it? That's you!"

"No, no. Absolutely not!" George attempts to recover the situation. "I grant you, it might bear a superficial resemblance but I've never been to Blackpool. I assure you."

"Well, maybe not. But anyway, it's about time I was getting home. My parents will be getting worried and I want to say goodnight to my children." Kirsten gets off the bed and gets her coat.

"Kirsten, please believe me. That is not me and we were getting along so well. Please stay a little."

"No, really, I must be getting back. But thanks for a lovely evening." And as an afterthought, she says, unconvincingly "Perhaps we could do it again."

"Well, let me walk you back home," suggests George.

"No thanks. That is kind of you but it's no distance and I'll be very happy on my own." She goes to the door, opens it as quickly as she can and runs to the lifts putting on her coat as she does so. There is no lift there so she goes on to the stairs and almost trips and falls as she hurries down. She is swiftly across the foyer and through the main doors. The receptionist on duty looks up but barely gives her a glance. When fifty or so yards from the hotel she looks back but there is no one to be seen. She slows her pace to a normal walking speed.

George knows that if Kirsten gets to her parents' house, which is about half a mile from the hotel, he is going to be in serious trouble. She must be stopped. He grabs his coat and follows her steps along the corridor to the stairs then nips back to his case and from this he takes a short double edged knife. This is a remnant from his street gang days. He never carries it but usually has it accessible as a reassurance. He dashes down the stairs, walks quickly though the lobby and slips out after Kirsten into the night putting his coat on as he does so and turning up the collar.

Kirsten has only gone another eighty yards when George looks out from the doorway of the hotel. He ducks back into its cover until he sees Kirsten look round and then slow her pace. Then George crosses the street. Lengthening his stride to give maximum speed without apparently hurrying, quickly and silently he goes up the other side following, catching up and then passing Kirsten keeping his face hidden the while. Kirsten is aware of the figure on the other side of the street but pays little attention and does not regard it as a threat in any way especially when the figure turns in the opposite direction to her at the top of the street ahead.

However, although George turns away from her, into the next exit, he immediately crosses the road to the opposite side. He turns round so that when he next appears in Kirsten's view it will seem that he has just come out of that street. He crosses to her side of the road. Now he is walking very quickly towards her as she approaches her destination. She still does not sense a threat until the figure is nearly level with her. Then George turns towards her and is swiftly on her, dagger in hand.

The blow from him is swift and delivered with maximum power. Kirsten can scarcely raise a squeak before she collapses with a moan.

"I'm sorry," says George. "It's just our bad luck."

He removes the blade with some care, fearful that blood might splash onto him. Then he wipes the knife on her coat and walks briskly away back to the hotel leaving a dark shadowed heap slumped outside the apartment front door.

Chapter 9

There is no sleep for George this Saturday night. Back in the hotel, he returns to his room seizing a moment when the night porter is away from his post at the reception desk. As quietly as he can and as swiftly, he takes a towel from the rack in his bathroom and soaks it in a soapy solution he makes up in the bathroom sink. Then he cleans every article he has touched in his room. He knows that he must clear the hotel before morning or he might as well hand himself in to the police. He also knows that wiping away all fingerprints is itself an admission of guilt. He just has to hope that his cleaning will be totally effective.

As he does so, he curses his luck. How on earth did they get an identikit of him? Who had seen him? And if the person who had seen him enough to help construct an identikit, he could only presume that they also might have details of his car. Of course he could easily change the number plates again but he could not change the colour without a re-spray and all that would do would be to bring attention to himself. He now regrets that he had not wiped the Blackpool house clean of fingerprints instead of leaving them. Doing that would promote the conclusion that the death had been an accident or at least make positive identification of him impossible. Whatever the evidence possessed by the police, they obviously think the Blackpool death is at least suspicious if not an actual unlawful killing. But if the Blackpool fingerprints were to be associated with any other death, especially a murder such as he had just perpetrated, it would cause George a serious problem. It would spark a major manhunt.

The least he can do is to erase any evidence that Kirsten's host was himself and then he needs to get back to his bed and breakfast and keep a low profile until the police decide that the killer is no longer in the vicinity. So still cursing his luck George cleans on.

During the night, with the volume of the television on low, he watches late night news. His identikit picture is shown regularly but so far there has been no mention of his BMW car. So at least he has managed to keep that hidden Having his car free to take him around opens up other options now and as he works he goes through them.

His immediate thought is to clear out from Sheringham and head south and west of London. Somewhere where there is little likelihood that he will be seen or even that people will be looking for him. A second option will be to return to his father's house and give some story about why he must do so. This does not seem a great idea as his father will almost certainly refuse to house him and indeed will rouse his suspicions especially as he will probably have seen the television reports and pictures. Yet another possibility is to return to his bachelor pad in Manchester. There he can pick up his passport and then head abroad but he feels he is a long way from being prepared for that.

His last option is to stay where he is. The landlady at his B & B is unlikely to suspect him of being involved with the murder virtually on her own doorstep. With a bit of luck he will get back into the house while it is still dark and, come breakfast time, she will think that he has spent the whole night in his room. If he grows a beard for the next few days, this will help him disguise himself and he can also change his hairstyle. Thereafter he will just have to play it by ear.

George finishes cleaning and wiping surfaces and handles as best he can and then sneaks out of the hotel and back to his boarding house. There, using his key and making no noise, he creeps to his room and gets into bed. He lies awake for most of the rest of the night going over and over where he has gone wrong and what he must now do. Then, amazingly, just before dawn, he falls asleep.

A knock on the door. George wakes up in a state of shock and panic with his heart rate doubling in seconds. Can it be the police?

Chapter 10

On the Sunday after Christmas, Victor is lying in bed still half asleep and mulling things over in his mind. Although there was a friendly rugby match the previous day, he had ruled himself out because of the strong possibility that there would be requests for his presence due to sickness amongst his parishioners. Although this was something he routinely did in the Christmas season, it was very convenient this year as it allowed another week to pass after his ignominious dismissal from the pitch the previous Saturday. But it is about time that he got up. There is a service in half an hour so there is just time to get washed, shaved and dressed. This will be a communion service but without a sermon so there is no need for further preparation.

Sarah is by his side, still asleep and the boys are audible next door but relatively quiet as they play with the toys brought by a kind Santa Claus earlier in the week. The phone rings. Victor stretches sideways to a telephone on the bedside table.

"Elmstone vicarage."

"Is that Reverend Victor Wilson?" – a male voice, shaking a bit from old age perhaps, Victor guesses.

"Yes. Can I help you?"

"This is Adam Farrow."

Victor thinks hard. The name sounds familiar but he can't place where or why.

The man speaks again. "Kirsten's father."

"Of course, Mr. Farrow. It's good to hear you. Is everything all right?" As soon as he has said it, Victor knows it is a stupid remark to make. Why would the man be phoning at this time in the morning if there was not something wrong.

"Kirsten's dying," blurts out her father. "She was attacked last night just outside our house here and left for dead. The police think it was a mugging gone wrong. A neighbour was out walking a dog and came across her lying on the pavement. He called an ambulance immediately because he didn't know who she was in the dark. We'd gone to bed and we only found out when the police found her diary in her handbag and came round to see us after midnight." Victor can hear the man crying at the other end of the line. "Who would want to kill her?"

Victor is totally shocked such that he can barely think straight.

"Mr. Farrow, this is too awful. Where is Kirsten now? Would you like me to come to you now?"

"She's in our local hospital but they say we should be prepared for the worst. Yes, please, Victor. Heather and I both would. We're going to go back home now since we are both totally exhausted."

"I'll come as soon as I can." Victor takes the address details and puts the phone down. By this time Sarah is awake and aware that some major catastrophe has happened and is looking at Victor as he puts the telephone back on its stand. He has gone quite white and is, literally, speechless. He looks at Sarah aghast.

"Victor! What is it? What's wrong?"

"Kirsten has been attacked. That was her father. She's in hospital but at death's door." He can scarcely get his tongue round the words. "The police think it's a mugging gone wrong. What else could it be?"

Sarah's reaction is to burst into tears and both sobbing they hug each other for comfort.

Sarah turns on the local radio news and television together. The radio is full of it but beyond the name of the victim, has no details. Victor is thinking hard. He knows that the church people will now be aware. News like this travels through the community in minutes and he knows he must make mention of it in the forthcoming service. In his little office he kneels down and calms himself as best he can. What can he say at a time like this to his congregation that will not be totally banal but which will help them see this event against the background of their religion. He makes a few notes and then heads for the church. Sarah follows with the two boys.

Inside the church Alan is playing the sort of extemporary music at which he is so proficient on the organ. Victor goes and stops him.

"We've got a major problem," he says. "I've just had a call from Kirsten's father in Sheringham. Kirsten was attacked last night. Now she's dying in hospital. It has been on all the local radio and television"

Alan is obviously unaware of what has happened and is as stunned as Victor himself was.

"No hymns or anything sung at all, I think," says Victor.

"Victor. I couldn't play a note now anyway." Alan is in shock, choking with emotion.

"I think I shall talk for a few minutes and then we shall have some prayers for Kirsten."

Victor comes slowly from his seat to the front of the chancel. Word has spread though the village and the church is packed as much as for the Christmas Eve midnight service.

"Help me, Lord" he prays silently.

"We are gathered together to think about our dear friend Kirsten who, as we all now know, has been brutally attacked while on a brief holiday to her parents in Sheringham. We must pray for her and for the doctors and nurses who are attending her that they will do their utmost to help her. If God still performs miracles, then we can pray for one to happen now.

"The question we must all be asking is - Why? Why should a young, beautiful woman be taken away? How can God allow this evil to happen? What is the point in believing in God if this is what happens to those who love him? My friends, I believe the biggest mistake we can make in our Christian beliefs is to think that this is in any way God's will being done. That this is achieving, in some mysterious way, God's will. That we must submit ourselves to God's will. Too often we hear that the evil that happens must be God's will, as if it is part of some master plan for our benefit and eventual salvation. To that I can only say – "what sort of a God do you believe in?" Do you honestly believe that the evil that we have just witnessed is fulfilling any aims or objectives of our loving God – our loving Jesus? When we pray in the Lord's Prayer that God's will be done, we are praying for God's wishes to be done. God wishes us to love one another – love our neighbour as ourselves. If only we did.

"What we should never do is blame God for the evils of the world. Nor should we thank Him for the good things of life unless it be the good things that come from our love for each other.

"What we feel for Kirsten is love and it is that love which will sustain us and Kirsten in her desperate state now and in her passage in the next life if she should die - because we believe that there is a next life. And it is our love for Kirsten our love for her stricken parents and their love for her also which will sustain them all in their hour of grief and pain.

"So if you will pray, then pray that your love for Kirsten will strengthen her. That the surgeons and doctors who tend to her will give their maximum concentration to their efforts. And if you will, then pray for the assassin that he may see the evil of his ways, repent his wickedness and give himself up so that we and Kirsten's parents can know why he did this terrible thing.

"That is our firm belief," says Victor, "and it is my firm belief also that Kirsten, if she were to die now, would live on and would live in God's presence somewhere, somehow."

"Finally, I have been asked by Kirsten's parents to visit them and I intend to set out immediately after this service. I am sure that I carry with me your love and prayers."

Victor then says some prayers from the prayer book. He feels relief that one of the good things about liturgical religions is that there is a prayer for every occasion. They are usually short and to the point and say what has to be said more meaningfully than extemporary prayers. During his brief talk and the prayers there has been much silent and not so silent weeping. Afterwards much more weeping and embracing. Victor knows that in a small community such as they inhabit, the common grieving will be of great mutual support and he is thankful for it.

Victor stands at the church door as the congregation leaves shaking everyone's by the hand and embracing.

"Give our love to Kirsten and Kirsten's parents," is the universal message.

Alan is the last to leave. "Would you like me to go with you to Sheringham?" he asks. "It's going to be a lonely journey otherwise."

"Yes, please, Alan. I would appreciate your company very much."

An hour later they are on their way in Victor's car. Sarah has packed a bag for him so that he can stay overnight if necessary. On his way out of the village he picks up Alan. As the journey progresses and the meeting with the parents gets closer, Victor becomes calmer. Being with the recently bereaved is all too commonly a part of the job and, while never easy, there is a routine of phrase and action which puts them at ease with him. On the other hand, Victor is aware that Alan is becoming increasingly agitated.

"What's wrong, Alan," he asks. "Are you regretting coming? You don't need to come in with me, if you don't want to. It is going to be extremely harrowing and I myself am not looking forward to it."

Alan pauses for a minute or two. "No. I shall carry on with you if you'll have me."

"I think Adam and Heather Farrow will appreciate it. You can add your voice to the wishes that we're taking with us from the parish."

When they arrive at the Farrow's address they recognise it by the fact that there are two police cars parked on the street outside, black and yellow crime scene tape surrounding the area, and a policeman standing outside. There is a small crowd of a dozen or so people including what might be a newspaper reporter.

They stop as close as they can get and walk up to the policeman.

"Are you the Reverend Wilson, sir?"

"Yes. And this is Mr. Jones who is from our church in Elmstone. What's the news on Kirsten?"

"She has been taken up to Norwich. As I understand it, sir, she is still hanging on but Inspector Barnes will have the latest report. He is with Mr. and Mrs. Farrow and a lady constable, PC Clark, is with them also."

"And where are the girls?"

"They are with friends of Mr. and Mrs. Farrow nearby. But just go straight in, please, and take the stairs up to the first floor."

He lifts his handset and announces that Victor has arrived. Victor and Alan go inside.

The Farrow's apartment is in block facing the sea and a few hundred yards from a large redbrick hotel. There are no buildings at all on the other side of the street. They enter the main door to the block and climb some stairs to the first floor where another policeman is standing. He opens the apartment door and waves them in.

Inside, they enter the first room which is plainly the main sitting room. Kirsten's parents are sitting together on a sofa holding hands and the policewoman is standing near the window. A grey haired, middle aged man in plain clothes gets to his feet from where he was sitting opposite the parents. He greets Victor and Alan.

"I'm Detective Inspector Barnes," he announces.

Victor and Alan shake his hand and then go to the sofa. Adam Farrow gets up and Victor and he embrace each other. Victor can feel the man trembling. Then he goes to Heather and sinks to his knees and hugs her. She virtually collapses in his arms breaking into great heaving sobs which rack her body. It takes some minutes for her to calm down aided by the policewoman. Alan meanwhile embraces Adam Farrow.

Barnes speaks first. "I know you've come principally to support Mr and Mrs Farrow, but I would appreciate a little of your time before I leave you."

"Just give me five minutes alone with Mr and Mrs. Farrow and then I'll join you."

"I'll be in the kitchen," says Barnes as he leaves.

Victor goes over to the Farrows, kneels down again and takes a hand of each of them in his.

"Adam and Heather. There isn't much I can say to support you in your agony. Kirsten is a wonderful lady as you both know. She is a loving member of our little community in Elmstone and is loved by everyone. Only a week ago she was decorating our church for Christmas. It was a very happy occasion and Kirsten loved every minute. This morning at church instead of our normal service we just remembered Kirsten and all the happy times we had had together. Every single member of the church prayed for Kirsten's survival and for yourselves and asked Alan and me to give you their love and to tell you that they share in your grief.

"You are wondering why this has happened. There is no explanation of why Kirsten was attacked in this way. It is part of the immense evil which fills the world and always has. We can fight it when we see it and eliminate it if we can. But believe me when I say that only our love for each other and for our God whom we trust will conquer that evil.

"Will you join me in prayer?"

"Yes, please," says Adam.

Victor, using again words that have been used for centuries in this context, asks for the Lord to give comfort and peace to Adam and Heather and to watch over Kirsten and those who care for her. Even in this situation he cannot bring himself to ask God to save Kirsten. If Kirsten dies then God must be blamed for not answering prayer and he would rather not put God into that situation. Despite his faltering belief in the efficacy of prayer he will not tempt God.

He gets up off his knees and goes to the door.

"Alan, can I leave you with Adam and Heather for a minute."

Inspector Barnes is sitting at the kitchen table. "Have a seat, Vicar." He pauses.

"Vicar, Mrs. Woodhouse was brutally attacked outside her gate last night about 10.30. She was stabbed. For what it's worth, the way it was done makes it look as though the attack was a deliberate attempt to kill and not, as was first thought, a mugging gone wrong. There was no attempt to steal her handbag or anything inside it. A further point is that we do not know everything about what she had been doing. According to her parents she had met an old friend in the town and had agreed to meet him or her for dinner without saying who or where that would happen. However, our immediate enquiries have ascertained that this was at the Grand Hotel with a young man. The man in question had booked in to the hotel in a double room for himself and, so he said, his wife. He paid in advance with cash and gave some tale about having had to stop his cards. But this morning he had left the hotel without sleeping in the bed. No one knows when this was. And no one has seen him either before or since. We are trying to build up a picture of what he looks like but the hotel staff were more interested in the lady, who was looking gorgeous apparently, than in her male partner.

"How can I help?" says Victor.

"Well, did Mrs. Woodhouse have a friend in Elmstone who might have been here yesterday? A friend close enough for her to meet for dinner and a possible assignation in a hotel bedroom? It has got to be someone who knew her."

Victor is stunned. "No. I can't say there is anybody in that category – at least that I know of. I am shocked to hear it. And if there were such a man he would have been at church this morning. And I can't think of anyone over the last period who was particularly friendly and left the village some time ago. Since Kirsten was widowed she has been very much on her own. It is inconceivable that she would pick up someone in the street for a one night stand – totally impossible. I'm sorry."

Barnes gives a sigh of frustration. "Well, think on," he says. "Perhaps something will come to mind and if it does please contact us immediately."

"Alan and I will stay at least tonight. I take it that the Farrows will be going up to Norwich to be at Kirsten's bedside."

Barnes says "Yes but the doctors all feel that she will survive at least for a few days and she will be undergoing surgery for some hours. So we shall take the Farrows up there tomorrow."

"Good," says Victor. "We will come and see Adam and Heather tomorrow and then return to Elmstone. Do you know somewhere we can stay – not too expensive?"

"PC Clark will certainly help you. She's local."

That evening, having booked in at a local B & B near the apartment, Victor and Alan are having a meal together in a local pub which serves food even on a Sunday. Victor explains the police inspector's problem.

I agree with you," says Alan. "I could swear that there has been no stranger, at least around the church, for the last three months and certainly no one who would know Kirsten."

"Actually, on Christmas Eve there was a stranger at the midnight service. A young chap, obviously quite shy."

"I didn't see anyone," says Alan.

"You were otherwise engaged playing the organ."

"Yes, but when I wasn't I usually look around to see who's there and who isn't."

"Well, this man was sitting behind one of the rear pillars. I saw him when he was the last to come in - just as we were processing. Then when I was at the door after the service he sort of ducked out past me and avoided my handshake. Like I said, he was very shy."

Alan splutters in his beer and goes into a coughing fit.

Victor pats him on the back. "Are you all right, old man?"

Alan gasps. "Something went down the wrong way."

"Anyway," says Victor "I'm certain I've never seen the man before and therefore that there's no way that he is local to us."

"Absolutely," agrees Alan. "Well, Victor, let's turn in now and leave tomorrow morning. We'll go and see the Farrows and then we can be off home. You've done all you can for the moment."

"That's true. Now we are here, I would like to have a quick stroll along the coast. I do love the sea but now I'm ready for bed. Sleep well, Alan."

Chapter 11

"Morning Mr. Meredith. Are you all right?" A voice on the other side of the door.

Thank God, it's just the B and B owner, thinks George, who has broken out into a sweat.

"Yes, I'm just fine, thanks, Mrs Scott. I'll be down for breakfast in just two minutes."

"Well, you certainly slept well. Not shaving today, Mr. Meredith," is his landlady's first comment when George appears.

George laughs. "Do me a favour, Mrs. Scott. This is supposed to be a holiday for me so I intend to look scruffy, if you don't mind. I don't intend to start shaving and looking neat until after New Year's Day when I start work again."

Mrs. Scott giggles archly. "Well, you still look very dashing to me."

"Thank you, ma'am. You're too kind."

"And have you seen the news this morning, Mr. Meredith?"

"What news?" says George.

"A young lady was attacked last night not half a mile away from us here."

"How awful. Is she badly hurt?" asks George anxiously.

"Well. She's not dead but she's in intensive care and not expected to live."

"That's terrible," says George, "Especially in a peaceful place like Sheringham. I would have thought this would be a crime free zone. We'll just have to hope for the best."

But the badinage gives George food for thought. Mrs. Scott is plainly single although whether so by divorce or death he has had no indication. Also, although of uncertain age, she is not quite as youthful as George likes his women, a sexual liaison might have its advantages.

Sunday morning breakfast passes normally except for the fact that the tomato sauce with his fried bacon, sausage and egg is accompanied by a running commentary by Mrs Scott on the horrendous attack which has happened during the night. The local radio station is full of it and his landlady keeps George up to date with developments. These are minimal at the moment and are entirely conjecture along the lines that it is a mugging and robbery gone wrong. Little is said about where Kirsten had been or with whom and the subject of where George spent his evening also does not come up.

"That was lovely," says George after his hearty breakfast. "Seeing it's a sunny day, I think I shall have a walk along the coast this morning and maybe a snack somewhere."

"The coastal path goes alongside the golf course. It's a long time since I did it but the views from the cliff top are amazing or, if the tide is out, then you can actually walk along the shore. But put on plenty of clothes. It'll be cold."

"Excellent," says George enthusiastically. "I'll see you later."

"By the way," she adds, "if you like I can do a meal for you tonight. I was going to do liver and bacon for myself but I can make it for two just as easily."

"Mrs. Scott, that is very kind of you. And if you really wouldn't mind I would love to join you. That'll be something else to look forward to."

George is well pleased. On the Sunday after Christmas, there will not be many shops open where a strange face might be noticeable. Perhaps his luck is beginning to turn. He dons his coat and wraps a scarf round his neck and chin concealing the lower half of his face and sets out towards the town centre and spends much of the morning in exploring the town and out along the coast to the west. On the land side is the Sheringham golf course which stretches a mile and a half westwards along the coast before turning back towards the town. The land rises to a high point which is perhaps two hundred feet above the beach. At its highest point there is a Coastguard observation hut which stands sentinel-like over the surrounding land and sea. Next to it are some advertising boards which are loosely fixed to the ground. The hut cannot be seen from the shore immediately below but it dominates the scene and from there it is possible to see miles out to sea. On the land side, the complete golf course is laid out below and, inland from that, agriculture fields farmed mostly with livestock but the occasional arable crop. These are separated from the golf course by a railway line along which runs the Sheringham to Holt steam railway.

Certainly, the walk along the coast is enjoyable; the views across the North Sea unimpeded. Occasional boats are in sight from time to time. George can breathe deeply and stretch his limbs giving himself a feel-good experience. He returns to the town and has a snack at a pub near the harbour and later on returns to the house.

The evening meal with Mrs Scott (call me Beth) goes well. George (call me George) turns on the charm and the evening ends up with Beth asking "Are you warm enough, George? I can let you have another blanket."

"Yes, please, I am a bit cool."

She then adds nervously. "Or you could come into my bed if you like. It's a big double bed and that would be warmer for us both."

"Beth, I can think of nothing better."

Somewhat to George's surprise, the sex with Beth Scott is very enjoyable and leaves both of them exhausted. She is waiting for him with the blankets drawn up to her chin but when George pulls them back, he finds her completely naked. George takes off his pyjamas and as he climbs in beside her she switches off the bedroom light.

"I prefer feeling my way to seeing it," she murmurs as she sets out with enthusiasm and athleticism. George is impressed - she obviously knows what it is all about and, he guesses, has been deprived of it for many years since her husband died. George cannot help wondering if the poor man died of exhaustion. As George falls asleep he knows that he has acquired an ally who will defend him and, if necessary give him an alibi for the Saturday night. Hopefully, also, he will be able to stay in this house until after New Year.

The following day, Monday morning, George sets out again after a late breakfast. It is while he is strolling slowly along the main street and casually looking in the shop windows that he happens to look across the street. Two men are threading their way along the opposite pavement. With a heart stopping shock he recognises first of all his father and then, immediately, the Vicar of Elmstone. For the second time in less than a week, they make eye contact.

George does not have time to conjecture what they are doing in Sheringham. His first, guilty impulse is to escape and he turns immediately into the shop he is standing outside. It is a small supermarket and has three rows of shelves running the length of the shop. He goes down the left hand aisle heading swiftly to the back of the shop. Then he hears the door opening and is aware that the two men must have seen him and followed him. At the end of his aisle there is a door presumably into a rear storage area or staff room. George opens it as noiselessly as he can and slips through. As he closes the door, he looks back and glimpses his father coming into the far end of the aisle. His father may have seen him and he expects to hear a shout. None comes and George has no idea if he has been seen and recognised. He passes down another corridor of stacked boxes to a back entrance, lets himself out into a rear access road and then walks as quickly as he can back to the main street and relative safety.

In an alley further along the street he conceals himself out of sight of the supermarket doorway. He guesses now that their visit is closely connected to his attack on Kirsten. He definitely does not want to meet either of them. To do that will give rise to awkward questions. He suspects that his father has recognised him but has not reacted - probably feeling that a meeting will just raise embarrassing questions for both of them and therefore has deliberately done nothing to stop him escaping. Hopefully, the Vicar knows nothing at present but it won't take long for him to add two and two together and realise that George has something to do with Kirsten. George gives a little smile to himself. Maybe his father is on his side – at least at the moment. So maybe George is a chip off the old block after all and maybe the old block can be of more help to George yet. One thing is clear. The Vicar will have to be eliminated from the scene and if that means killing him, then that is the way it has to be.

So George keeps watch to see where the pair will go next. Suddenly, the hunted man becomes the hunter.

Chapter 12

Earlier on the Monday morning, Victor telephones the Norwich hospital to which Kirsten has been transferred. The news is that Kirsten is still on the critical list but so far is holding her own.

After breakfast, Victor and Alan pack, pay the bill and put their bags in the car before visiting the Farrows. Having said their farewells with promises to stay in close touch, they set off down the High Street walking towards the coast. Suddenly, Victor stops.

"Alan. I think I've just seen the chap we were talking about."

"Which chap?"

"The man who I saw in church on Christmas Eve. And I think he saw and recognised me because we made eye contact and then he turned away quickly and shot off somewhere - into that supermarket, I think."

"Are you sure?" says Alan.

"Not totally, but we definitely seemed to recognise each other. I'm going to find him." And Victor sets off with Alan following.

"What is he wearing?"

"Dark coat – no hat."

They enter the shop which has got several rows of shelves.

"You go that way and I'll do this alley," says Alan and goes to his left. Victor heads off to the right and they meet at the far end of the shelves.

"Anything your side?" asks Victor.

"No," says Alan. "No one remotely resembling who you described. I'll go round again and you stay at the door and keep watch."

Two minutes later they decide that they have missed the man and give up.

"That's very odd," ponders Victor. "I could have sworn that I saw him come in here. There's a door marked "Staff Only" going through to the back premises. There must be a rear entrance for deliveries so maybe he went that way."

"I certainly saw no one. Oh well, let's carry on with our walk and keep our eyes open," says Alan.

Reluctantly, Victor agrees and they continue heading towards the sea down the High Street to the sea front. There they turn left and head along the road parallel to the sea. There is a path leaving this road which goes underneath the main road pavement onto the shore.

"Tide's out," observes Alan. "Let's go along the beach."

They walk westwards along the beach which is largely shingle although the receding tide has revealed hard sand. On their left, the sea stretches over the horizon apparently to infinity. Above them on their right as they walk, the white cliffs tower rising to about 200 feet above them before reducing in height to perhaps half that amount.

"I like looking at the sea," remarks Alan as they proceed along the coast. "I find the perpetual motion mesmerising."

"I'll stick to the cliffs," says Victor. "You can usually get a good idea of the geological history if you look closely."

Alan groans. "Once a scientist, always a scientist. Have you no romance? Doesn't the sea make you think of foreign lands? Don't you have any poetry in your soul?"

Victor grins and heads to the cliffs.

From the edge of the water, Alan turns and looks towards Victor and the cliffs behind. The Coastguard hut catches his attention for standing beside it is a figure in a dark coat. As Alan continues to watch the figure approaches the edge of the cliff and looks over. It is George and he is clutching a large flat object. It is too far for eye contact to be made but Alan is sure that George has followed them and, judging by the attitude of his body, is looking at him - focussing on him. Victor is directly below George but Alan cannot see what George is hoping to do nor why he has been eluding them. He very much fears that the attack on Kirsten has something to do with it but cannot bring himself to believe that George is the attacker.

He raises his arm acknowledging that he has seen and recognised George. Within seconds a large object is flung over the edge of the cliff and plummets towards Victor. Alan involuntarily holds his breath paralysed by what he is seeing and unable to affect it. Just above Victor, the object strikes a projecting rock on the cliff face which throws it outwards and it crashes to the sandy beach inches from him. It comprises two large boards attached together but, other than that, Victor cannot tell what it is or where it came from. One thing is sure, however. If it had struck either of them, it would have been fatal.

Victor is shaken by this but reacts quickly.

"What the hell!" he yells and quickly runs away from the side of the cliff looking backwards and upwards as he goes.

"Did you see that?" he shouts to Alan.

"Not really," says Alan.

George is still looking over the edge and is not quick enough to pull back before Victor runs into view. Victor just sees the head and shoulders of George

"I think that was the man we saw in the town," shouts Victor to Alan.

"It might have been," says Alan.

Victor shouts "I'm going to get him." and he sets off back along the beach towards the town running as hard as he can. It is slow going because of the sand and shingle as he aims for the underpass they came through minutes earlier. Alan follows on behind as fast as he can but is falling behind Victor all the time.

George starts to hurry back towards the town, running when he can but slowing to a quick walk whenever he passes someone hoping thus not to draw attention to himself. When he gets to the footpath underpass there is as yet no sign of the vicar but he presses on as fast as possible. He reaches the first corner and turns into it but as he does so he looks back and sees Victor emerging from the underpass tunnel.

"Shit," says George in exasperation and sets off again at an increased pace. He then takes two more turns before entering his own road, runs to his boarding house and goes in. He gets to his room and collapses onto his bed – chest heaving. Although strong, George is not very fit and the extended effort has winded him. Then he hears the front door opening and footsteps coming swiftly up the stairs. He goes to his suitcase and takes out his knife.

Victor is moving at much the same speed as George. He comes out from the underpass stops to look back up the hill to his right. There is no sign of his attacker. He guesses when he does not see the man that he is now ahead of him going into town and has taken one of the side roads. Although he loses time by stopping to look along those other side streets, he gets to the end of George's street just in time to see him disappear into a house. Behind him Alan is just able to keep Victor in sight.

Victor races down the street to the house, which is marked by a B & B sign on the gatepost, turns in to the pathway and bursts in through the front door. A lady comes out from the door at the end of the corridor.

"Where has that man gone who came in just now?" he shouts.

"Do you mean Mr. Meredith?" asks the lady.

"If that's his name, yes.

"I'll go and see if he's in," says the lady heading towards the stairs.

"Don't bother." Victor heads up the stairs, two at a time, leaving the landlady open-mouthed behind. The first door he opens shows an empty room. The second door opens to reveal a man standing with a knife in his hand. Victor has no time for introductions.

"I think I know who you are," says Victor "and I think I know what you've done. It's time to give yourself up to the police."

George gives a mirthless laugh. "You think so, do you. Well, bugger off Mr. Vicar and mind your own business."

"Look. You may think you can kill me, but you can't kill my friend. He'll be going to the police now anyway."

George laughs. "No he won't," he says.

"And if you do kill me you'll have to kill your landlady also."

"No I won't," repeats George.

"Look," says Victor "Give up before you've ruined more lives."

"Don't preach at me, Vicar. Keep that for your sermons." And as he speaks he launches himself at Victor slashing at him with the knife. Victor instinctively jumps backward avoiding George's lunge but in so doing he hits the dressing table chair which is right behind him. He falls over backwards over the chair but ends up on the other side of the chair from George. He rolls sideways to his knees quickly and gets quickly to his feet. He grasps the chair and raises it in time to parry the next slash from George. George's arm hits the chair and the knife is knocked free and skitters across the floor to near the window.

George turns and dives for the knife but Victor is as quick and takes him round the knees in a rugby tackle which puts George on his face on the floor but with the knife just outside his reach. George gets a leg free from Victor's grip and tries to kick Victor on the head. He catches Victor a glancing blow and Victor's grip slackens giving George the opportunity to get a foot closer to the knife. Victor now has a good two handed grip on George's right foot and he twists the ankle has hard as possible. The pain is excruciating to George and to reduce the torque he jack-knifes downwards to punch Victor's head. This gives Victor the opportunity to move his grip further up Victor's back and get a hand round George's chin. The two men are thrashing around now on the floor, their faces contorted with the effort and this brings George to within reach of the knife. He is straining every muscle to reach it and Victor is applying his maximum effort to restrain him. It is now a question of sheer physical strength. George's foot comes in contact with the leg of dressing table. Victor is amazed at George's strength and he can now sense that George is getting some extra leverage against the leg of the dressing table and is about to grasp the knife. He knows that if this happens the fight will be over. Both men are at exhaustion point when suddenly there is a sharp crack. Victor is unsure what has caused the noise and guesses that they have broken a piece of furniture. Then he feels George relax. Perhaps it is a ruse to make Victor relax his grip so Victor keeps the pressure on.

After a few seconds, Victor realises that George is unconscious and he himself relaxes and rolls away. Just then he hears the door open. He turns towards it. Alan is standing at the door. In his hand is one of the silver topped walking sticks from the hall hat stand. His face is a mask of fury and he lashes Victor across the head stunning him with the blow. Victor lying on the floor looks at Alan with amazement as the stick rises and then falls again.

"Damn you," shouts Alan.

The shock of this statement freezes Victor in disbelief. And as the blow falls, Victor knows in that instant that he is going to die. His last thought is – now I shall know what heaven is like.

Chapter 13

Victor's first awareness is of pain – pain primarily in his head which is so fierce that he is barely aware of pain in his neck and arms. His first conscious thought is that, if this is heaven, he is definitely not impressed. He then tries to open his eyes but no amount of concentration enables him to do this. His eyelids feel as though they are stuck firmly together. He is aware of movement around his body and concludes that there are things or even people around him. He hears murmuring voices and this persuades him that he is probably still alive. Something very cold is placed on his forehead and the shock of this overcomes his eye blockage and the eyelids shoot open. He is looking at a female face - a middle aged lady with Harry Potter spectacles and a white hat on her head. This confirms his suspicions – this is not an angel and he is not in heaven. He feels intense disappointment.

"So we're awake are we? How are we feeling?"

Victor thinks that she may be feeling fine but he is feeling, if not dead, at least at death's door. He groans in response to this rhetorical query.

The non-angel gazes into his eyes as if searching for something. She nods her head approvingly and moves away.

"Well, he seems to be all right," the lady says. "I'll just get a doctor to confirm his state and whether there is any concussion. Almost bound to be." She moves away and her face is replaced by another. It is Sarah.

"Can I kiss him?"

"Yes, but gently."

Sarah kisses Victor on his forehead.

"Was that sore?"

"Just a little," whimpers Victor. "Just a little lower please."

The next kiss is on the lips.

"Was that better?"

A faltering "Yes."

"Again?"

Again a whispered "Yes, please."

By this time Sarah suspects that Victor is making the most of this. "You chancer!" she accuses him. "There's nothing wrong with you."

"I'm afraid there is," says a voice behind. A doctor has arrived. "Your husband has had a very severe blow to his skull. We still have to make sure that there is no permanent brain damage so, please, no excitement."

"What sort of excitement?" asks Sarah.

The doctor ignores this remark and makes another examination of Victor's eyes.

"Hmm. I think he'll be alright. Please don't tire him. What he needs now is some genuine sleep." he says and moves away.

Sarah is back leaning over the bed. Victor's memory is slowly returning.

"How long have I been unconscious?"

"About thirty six hours."

"How is Kirsten doing?"

"She's doing well - as well as can be expected. She's off the critical list but still in intensive care."

"Thank God," mutters Victor unaware of the way this thought conflicts with his beliefs. He is silent for a moment as he gathers this thoughts.

"Where's Alan?" he asks.

Sarah hesitates. Eventually she mutters "He's disappeared."

"He hit me didn't he? Why did he hit me?"

"Because the man you were fighting was his son. His name was George and he passed himself in Sheringham as George Meredith. The police are fairly certain that he was the man who killed that woman in Blackpool. They found matching fingerprints on the chairs they were sitting on at dinner. Do you remember – they were showing an identikit picture of him on TV and they think that Kirsten probably recognised him and that she was killed to prevent her reporting him."

Victor is quite slow assimilating this.

"And where is this Meredith fellow, then?"

"I'll tell you later."

"Tell me now!" Victor speaks firmly and the effort gives him a violent burst of pain in his skull. He waits for three or four minutes till this subsides.

"Tell me," he repeats fearing the worst.

"He's dead."

"Dead?"

Victor again tries to recall the events immediately prior to his unconsciousness but he does so with a growing sense of dread.

"What happened?"

There is no way that Sarah can avoid this and be honest with her husband.

"There's no easy way of putting this," she says. "You killed him."

"I killed him?" Victor questions in disbelief. "How?"

"You broke his neck."

"O God!" and, unable to cope with this shocking revelation, Victor faints back into the safety of unconsciousness again.

It is an hour later that Victor wakes again. Sarah is still there watching over him and the memory of the last piece of information is there also.

"I killed a man," mutters Victor. "How could God do this to me?"

"You know perfectly well and I've heard you say it dozens of times – God had nothing to do with it. George Meredith was an evil man – a criminal. And he was trying to kill you. He died as you were defending yourself," responds Sarah. "There's no way anyone is going to blame you. The man had already killed one person and tried to kill Kirsten. The police aren't going to take any further action."

"Alan will blame me," says Victor. "And I don't blame him for attacking me. I would have done the same. What's happened to him?"

"He took your car and drove back to Elmstone. He obviously picked up some stuff from his house and then left your car there, took his own car and left that at the railway station. Nobody has a clue about his whereabouts."

At this point the doctor returns to the room. "Mrs. Wilson," he says. "You really must let your husband rest. His mental and physical strength is in overload. We must let him rest now and deal with what has happened."

Sarah and the doctor leave the room with only the nurse in attendance. Victor closes his eyes and within seconds is once again fast asleep.

A couple of hours later, Victor is again awake. This time the morphine he received earlier has taken effect and his head is almost clear of pain – but not his mind. The enormity of what he has done is almost too much for him to bear. Sarah is still with him.

"How do you feel now? As bad as you look"

Victor looks puzzled. Sarah continues "You have a pair of record breaking black eyes."

But Victor has more important things on his mind. "Sarah, I can't get out of my mind that I've done a terrible thing." He pauses.

"I really don't think I can continue with my ministry" he says. "I've been thinking about this and it seems to me that I've killed a man and so I've cut myself off from God and I'm in no position now to act as a minister of God. I'm sorry, sweetheart, but I don't think I can continue."

"Victor – just stop this. Stop this instantly. You are just wallowing in self-pity and that doesn't suit you at all. You know perfectly well that he was trying to kill you and that he had already killed one other person. And what's more, you are good at the job – and I mean really good. Do you want to throw all that away? If you want to bring God into it, why not take the view that He is testing your strength."

"Maybe so" replies Victor. "But the fact remains that I have taken a human life. And the sixth commandment is unambiguous – Thou shalt not kill. No ifs or buts. And the whole ethos of our religion is to love those who hate you. Do good to those who ill treat you. Turn the other cheek and so on. To be true to my beliefs, I should have let him kill me."

"And then go on to kill other people?" asks Sarah. "You're talking rubbish. Surely there is a greater good here. A lesser of two evils?"

"But that's just rationalising to justify what you want to do rather than what we ought to do. What we are told to do."

"And you are just rationalising to justify your self-pity. Well, go and talk to someone else about it," suggests Sarah. "The bishop perhaps. For the moment let's just get home to our family. The boys are dying to see you. That will give you a dose of reality if nothing else does. I've got the car here, now that the police have released it, so we can go right now if the doctor agrees."

"And, by the way, I have another bit of information for you."

"Oh, yes?" says Victor somewhat doubtfully.

"We are going to have two extra children for the next few months. I've offered to take Jenny and Lucy until Kirsten is back in business so we'll have a house full when you get home. Now, I've got some clean clothes for you. So let's head for home as soon as you get signed off by the doctor here."

Chapter 14

"But what has happened to the virtues of forgive and forget?" demands Victor.

"What's happened to forgive and forget?" repeats the Bishop. "Forgiving is the easy part – it's forgetting that is the problem. And I'm sorry to say it, Victor, but the fact that you have just killed a man with your bare hands is very difficult to forget." The Bishop is bald, bland and, usually, benevolent. He has only been consecrated for six years and is, reputedly, interested in creating and preserving links to the surrounding society.

Victor is in the Bishop's palace in his study sitting in front of the desk with the Bishop himself seated behind in the position of authority - a headmaster with a pupil or at best a young member of his staff. It is reliably rumoured that the Bishop has married into money and the room is a demonstration of that. The quality of the antique furniture, the art on the walls and the Greek icon, a triptych mounted on the wall under its own illumination, show wealth in an understated way. It is also rumoured that his wife's connections were material in his elevation to the episcopacy - but the clergy are no more immune to scurrilous rumours than any other profession.

It is only the second time that Victor has been in this inner sanctum, the first being when the previous incumbent was there and just before Victor was selected for the benefice in Elmstone. His other previous encounters with the Bishop were when he was inducted into the parish and at the ordination in the cathedral of new priests when most of the clergy in the diocese turn out in support.

Word has come through from the diocese headquarters that Victor has been given "gardening" leave and instructed not to participate in services for the time being. The implied reason for this is to allow him time to recover. Indeed, there is good reason for this since Victor has been suffering from sleepless nights and when he does sleep – terrible nightmares. He frequently wakes up sweating heavily, threshing the bedclothes and fighting for his life against unknown assailants. Sarah has been tempted to leave their double bed for the spare room because of a very real danger of being hurt but does not want to do so. So far she has been wakened herself and has managed to rouse Victor before this has happened.

He is also suffering bouts of black depression where he questions more deeply than ever before, his beliefs, his career and all his relationships. Sarah, whose training has been as a psychologist, is convinced that he is suffering from post-traumatic stress disorder similar to that suffered by soldiers who have been in battle situations.

Victor's suggestion that he is recovered, or at least sufficiently recovered, to take services and will benefit from so doing, has been brushed aside. He should do nothing until he has seen the Bishop. And here he is now – in the lion's den, he thinks.

"But everyone knows that first of all he was trying to kill me, secondly that he was a murderer and thirdly that he would then have killed the landlady and also, or so I believed, Alan Jones."

"Yes, yes. Of course I know that. But it's the atmosphere of violence that now is attached to you. People feel threatened when they should feel comforted and reassured."

"I've always felt that people felt reassured by my size. Who feels threatened?" asks Victor. "It's the Derbyshires, isn't it? They have never liked me."

"The Derbyshires are certainly of that view and they tell me that they are speaking for many others in your parish. They also tell me that some of your beliefs are distinctly non-conformist. But that apart, I think your position there is untenable. I'm sorry Victor. I have spent many hours thinking and praying about this and, believe me, it is with great reluctance that I have reached the decision."

Victor is devastated and sits silent for a minute or two.

He tries again. "But I've been successful, haven't I? The church attendances have doubled. Our income has trebled. I've started a Youth Club, a toddlers Group, a Sunday School, a men's meeting and so on. The Church is actually winning in Elmstone. This incident will be forgotten in a year or so."

"My judgment is that it won't be and that your continuation will bring harm to the parish and the things you have started. I'm sorry, Victor, but you'll have to go. And I'm suspending you for the moment until we can sort out what to do with you."

Victor says "My Lord, I thought you would be my friend. You say as much to every new priest in your diocese. Now you've turned against me. I don't know who my true friends or neighbours are anymore. Who is my neighbour now? Your actions are making me doubt my very faith. And," he hesitates, "I've been having doubts anyway."

"What doubts?"

"Around the nature of faith. I am always conscious of St. Paul's definition of faith. "Faith is the substance of things hoped for, the evidence of things not seen". I can understand the "hoped for" element of faith – what I have trouble with from time to time is the evidence part of the equation. As a scientist I constantly look for evidence – it is the very essence of the scientific process – and from my perspective, particularly with what you've just been saying - evidence seen or unseen is in fairly short supply."

He pauses then continues "I sometimes hope that the example of the clergy in the Church of England will be a shining example of the Christian life. But I see them as interested in material wealth as the rest of the community. Nothing seems to give some of my colleagues as much satisfaction as buying and showing off a new car. And when I see the parade of the senior clerics of our church in their ridiculous robes and headgear, clutching their bejewelled staffs and crooks, I really wonder what it is all about."

"We are only human," replied the Bishop. "It's important to engage with the larger community and if we all wore hair shirts and open sandals I doubt that that would be the case."

Victor, now he is in his stride, is continuing without a break. "And you, my Lord, are a good example of what is wrong. The very fact that you live in a "bishop's palace" and are addressed by your subjects as "My Lord" is contrary to the Christian ethic of humility and service."

"Well, these are traditions of the Church," replies the Bishop, getting more than a little testy. "It's true that sometimes our example is not what it should be. And as for the horrid happenings you have been involved in – well, these things happen, Victor. They are unfortunate but we must consider that in some way they are working out God's purpose and God's will for us. And God will have a purpose for you too. You must learn to put yourself in God's hands."

Victor can contain himself no longer. He does not know whether to laugh or cry.

"God's purpose" he shouts in frustration. "So the murder in Blackpool, Kirsten's murderous attack, my killing of Alan's son, the enormous pain to Alan himself and to me and to Sarah and all the parish – is all part of God's plan. It just cannot be so. I cannot believe that this is any part of God's purpose. I will not believe that our God, our God of love, wills any of this as a purpose or a plan. In fact, my Lord, I don't really believe that our God has a plan. Don't we make our own plans and hope that they are in line with principles of belief and behaviour that were laid down by Jesus? Don't you think I have suffered enough?"

The Bishop breaks in. "Victor, my son. Two things occur to me. First – the violence of your outburst just now on top of the incident on the rugby field, which has come to my notice, demonstrates that you are at heart prone to violence and as such you should be questioning whether you are in the right career in the Church of England. Secondly, it seems to me that you are developing your own creed of beliefs away from the traditional creed of the Church. Again, I question whether you are in the right place. Now, Victor, go home now before you say something you will regret. In the meantime, I shall be thinking and praying about you and consulting my colleagues in the Church. There is no hurry to leave the vicarage. It'll take us some time to get your replacement so, within reason, take as much time as you want. Talk to

Sarah, pray to God about it and we shall discuss later what the best path for you and your family will be."

The Bishop bows his head over his hands resting on his desk. "Let us pray together," and shuts his eyes. Victor bows his head also but his eyes remain open.

"Lord," the Bishop intones, "help us to see the way of truth, the way you wish for your church and for Victor and his family. Amen"

"Oh, Lord," says Victor in response, "Help us to see the way of love so that we may love those who harm us and spitefully use us. Amen."

"Amen," repeats the Bishop.

The Bishop stands and holds out his hands for Victor to shake. "I can see that you are bitter and angry about this and I can only ask you to reflect upon what I've said."

And Victor is certainly bitter. Through no fault of his own and in trying to apprehend a murdering criminal, he has ruled himself out of a job in the Church and, thus condemned, has gained himself a reputation which will probably stay with him for life.

He feels that this should be a reason for giving him support, sympathy and some form of counselling in how to deal with it. Instead of this, he has lost his career, the one thing which may bring him back to normality. He is tempted to pursue the argument with the Bishop but senses that to do so will only alienate him further. That will only be to his detriment and so he keeps his mouth shut.

As he is returning to the village, Victor feels the strongest sense of disappointment, rejection and injustice of his life. As he approaches he sees the village in a new light – not as a collection of houses and people he will have to leave but as a living community which he loves and which is effectively throwing him out.

Sarah is waiting for him at their front door. As he walks in from the car, she can see that he is upset and hugs him close. He hugs her too for several minutes and as he does so he feels her warmth and love soaking into him.

Finally she whispers. "How did it go?"

"Awful. We're out of a job."

"What – just like that?"

"More or less. We're not quite being kicked out onto the street. But that is what it amounts to."

Sarah listens in disbelief as Victor recounts what has been decided and the reasons for the effective destruction of his career.

"I think, to be honest, that what's hurting me most is that I've lost the game here – and, as you well know, I don't like losing – at anything, least of all my job."

"Jesus Christ probably saw himself as a loser," says Sarah. "And maybe people see you as a loser, too. But to my mind, you've met the conflict between Christianity and reality. Theoretically you should have let George get away with it but, if you had, other people would have been at risk and that would have been the evil thing to do. Should this country have succumbed to Hitler? It's the old conundrum "is there such a thing as a just war? And there is no excuse for Flora Derbyshire to ruin your life with her allegations of how the village is against you. I've come across no such feelings in the village. I'm very, very angry at her."

And when Sarah gets angry she gets quite livid. The colour drains from her face and she is in fighting mode. Her family know that in this mood she is to be avoided as her temper can be quite fearsome. It can be said of Sarah that she does not lose her temper often but when she does she loses it in a big way.

"That bitch Flora Devonshire," she grits out. "Right. I'm going to sort her out!"

"Don't waste your time," interjects Victor. "It won't make any difference. It's all fixed."

"You can turn the other cheek if you like," says Sarah. "I don't have to!." And Sarah storms out of the house.

Chapter 15

The Derbyshire's house is a large detached house built not in the traditional local flint and brick but in stone imported from quarries in Lincolnshire and is certainly one of the most expensive in Elmstone. It has an imposing porticoed front door. Sarah walks up the drive towards the garage and, skirting bare flowerbeds, across a pebbled path to the door. There she keeps her finger on the house bell continuously until the door opens. John Derbyshire arrives quickly and when he spots Sarah he visibly pales as the blood drains from his face.

"Which of you has been telling tittle tattle to the Bishop?" she enquires peremptorily.

John stammers "I'll just get Flora" and beats a hasty retreat. Sarah is left standing on the doorstep of the Derbyshire's house. She is incandescent with rage. Hell's fury is as nothing compared with a woman defending attacks upon her own mate. A couple of minutes later Flora, taking her time, arrives with arms folded across her ample chest ready for war.

Sarah delivers her prepared opening salvo.

"How dare you? How dare you go to the bishop with a catalogue of lies about my husband? Sheer fabrications about how he is regarded in the parish. You've never liked us and now you are viciously and deliberately destroying him.

"You snake," she spits. "You viper. You know that Victor has been the best thing for this parish for years and now through no fault of his own, he has been dismissed from the job he has done so well. How dare you, and how can you be so cruel as to tell those lies?"

"Mrs Wilson, there have been no lies. I've merely stated the truth which is that you husband has killed, in fact murdered, a man and that alone has caused him to lose all credibility in the parish."

"Credibility with whom?" shouts Sarah.

"Many people have said as much to me."

"Oh yes? Who exactly?"

"I've no intention of naming names for you to go and shout at people. You'll just have to take my word for it."

"I don't take your word for it. The truth is that you have resisted all the positive changes that Victor has made and you resent his success. You have no supporters but you have the gall to go to the Bishop and present yourself as a representative of the parish against your vicar. I shall go to the Bishop and demand that he carries out a full enquiry to establish that your accusations are false."

"You may do what you like, Mrs. Wilson. But if you do, that itself will split the village down the middle. I'll see to that. And if that happens, what will you have gained? Your husband's position will still be untenable and he will still have to leave. Why don't you face it? Your husband is quite unsuited to the job!"

"What?"

"All that tosh about prayers being a waste of time – not achieving anything. It's time he got down on his knees and did a bit of praying for himself."

Sarah is so staggered by this blatant misrepresentation that she is speechless.

"And another thing." Flora is now in full flow. "You're not much of a Christian yourself, are you? Do you think you're going to go to heaven? You're just an intellectual snob, you are. Just because you've been a university teacher you think you're superior. Well, get back to your university. You're no use here."

"Go to heaven?" replies Sarah. "If people like you are going to heaven – I don't want to be there!"

To that statement, Flora Derbyshire has no reply. She turns white, steps back and slams the door in Sarah's face.

"She was ready for me, Victor. And what's more – she really hates me. Hates both of us, I think."

Sarah has returned home and once inside the house has collapsed onto a settee, weeping. Victor is beside her holding her hand and looking concerned into her eyes.

"How come she was ready? How is that possible?"

"Oh, Victor. The whole village knows what is going on. Flora Derbyshire told everyone who would listen that she was going to the Bishop. Sally in the Co-op told me. Plenty of people were ready to agree with her – although mostly folk who never go to church. Not many of them would support her but not many would be prepared to tell her that to her face. It's like the bible says – "They all began to make excuse" or "walked by on the other side of the road"."

"So Flora is right then, is she?"

"To the extent that the action she's taking is going to split the village and the longer that the issue lasts the deeper will be the split. We neither of us want that, do we, Victor? You will never be forgotten here for the work that you've done and in due course I'm sure that Flora will be made to regret what she's done."

"In this world or the next?" queries Victor.

"Ah" says Sarah. "That's a good point. I don't think I made the situation any better by telling her that if she was going to heaven I didn't want to go there myself."

Victor looked stunned then goes to Sarah and hugs her close. Then he starts to laugh.

"Oh, dear. What would I do without you?" he murmurs into her ear. "I do love you, you know."

Sarah starts to laugh as well.

"You should have seen her face," she splutters. "I really feel sorry for John." And they both burst into peals of laughter.

When they have subsided back to normality, Victor says "I'm just reluctant to admit defeat to her and to the Bishop."

"Ah, that's your aggressive nature coming out. It's like your rugby. Sometimes you've got to admit that you are defeated. And in this case we are the losers. The final whistle has been blown and we've lost. It may be unjust but I think we have just got to move on and fight another day."

"But we know it's unjust," says Victor. "We know that the Bishop should be supporting us and not abandoning us. For our faith shouldn't we fight on?"

"We wouldn't win – but there's one consolation."

"What's that?"

"You're in good company."

"How do you mean?"

"Look what happened to Jesus. They killed him. But then it happened that he rose again and here we are two thousand years later and he's still around."

Victor gives a sad smile. "You're correct. All right, where do we go from here?"

Sarah stands back and looks up at Victor.

"I've got a plan," she says.

Chapter 16

"Well, has my plan worked then? It's coming up nearly two years since the great trauma so you ought to have an opinion by now."

It is a Friday evening at the end of a busy week for Sarah and Victor and they are sitting in the kitchen of their new house in Norwich having a cup of tea before preparing the evening meal.

"All right, clever clogs," says Victor with a grin. "After that last interview with the Bishop, I must admit I thought my world had collapsed. But now? Well now I'm happier than I ever thought I'd be outside the Church. I do enjoy teaching physics to A-level students and the others. I don't seem to have the same discipline problems as some of the other staff which helps. Mind you, playing rugby at top club level and having the nickname of "Killer" amongst the pupils is no hindrance. Also, it does help having colleagues that I can call friends. I can share problems and experiences with them too – and they are a good bunch although there is the odd exception. It's also good that there are no arguments in physics like there are in religious dogma. And there are plenty of kids who have the enquiring minds I love to engage with." Victor gets up and replenishes his cup of tea.

"Another difference" he goes on "is that you know as a teacher when you have been successful. You know when your pupils pass their exams. You also know when they fail and that means that you have failed in some degree also. There's an enormous satisfaction when I get a student or group to understand a difficult concept and equally when they fail, I have got to ask why and what I could have done better. With religion, you have no such measure. People may say that they believe but there is unlikely to be any proof. Look at Alan Jones. Wouldn't we have said that he was a true Christian and yet there must have been a shady past which we never got close to. The only downside of my career now is that it is much harder work. I can't stop and have a cup of tea when I want. It's non-stop unrelenting pressure throughout the whole day."

"I feel the same about the lecturing staff and the students in the university," agrees Sarah. "Also I've got friends there unlike any in Elmstone apart from Kirsten. It was always the problem with Elmstone wasn't it? You had me and Alan to some extent whom you could bounce your problems off but ultimately you were on your own and it was a lonely life. And I, at least, can never forgive the Bishop for what he did to you."

"Yes, I find it difficult too. I suppose he had his point of view and it was to some extent justified – but he was too easily persuaded by the Derbyshires and did little to establish how much their views were representative. Maybe it was part of God's great plan."

Sarah knows perfectly well that Victor is pulling her leg and responds with a similar tongue in cheek remark. "Bound to have been." she says. "And don't forget the good news about Kirsten. If she hadn't met the consultant in the hospital, she would not be happily married again and living within half a mile of us now. Jennifer and Margaret are over the moon at the thought of a new baby on the way. So other good things have come out of this. But, talking of Alan, have you heard any news as to what happened to him?"

"Not a whisper. I withdrew all charges against him and I don't see how he could be unaware of that otherwise there would be a police hunt for him. He must be aware that there is nothing hanging over him so it's all very odd."

"Mind you, it would have been very difficult for them to find him," says Sarah. "I don't think we had any photographs of him and neither apparently had anybody else."

"And we never had any idea of how he got his money – and he seemed to have plenty. He was generous in his giving to the church and the rugby club – although he always paid in cash. Never, as far as I know by cheque or direct debit. I did hear that his house had been sold but done through a solicitor who refused to reveal his whereabouts. Perhaps his money was all illegally obtained."

"I can't believe that of Alan," says Sarah vehemently. "He has always seemed basically a decent honest man. He certainly loved his rugby – I wonder if he watches it at all these days."

"Talking of which I have a big game tomorrow. Against my old club – which should be interesting."

"Will some of your pupils turn up to watch?" enquires Sarah.

"Yes, I'm sure some of the boys I coach will be there. That's another aspect of my life now that I enjoy. No doubt they'll be hoping to see whether the stuff I tell them works in practice." Another aspect of Victor's happiness is that he is involved with coaching the school rugby team as an after-school activity.

This is part of the success of Sarah's plan – for both of them to go into teaching – Sarah in University in Norwich and Victor in a modern academy in the same city. Their house, bought at a point of the housing market when both prices and mortgage rates were low, can just be afforded by what they had saved, some help from Victor's parents and on their combined salaries. It is out on the west side of the city and both boys attend a nearby primary school with the next level of academy school also close by. Victor plays rugby for one of the Norwich clubs and has managed to get into the first XV. At least there is no clash with church weddings to distract him. What Victor does miss is taking the church services, particularly when he was the celebrant at communion. This and the peace which he encountered within the church building itself. The nearest church is only a couple of streets away and within easy walking distance, so Victor goes regularly but takes no part in the services. A large, grassed play park is also quite close at hand and there Victor plays with his two boys.

Sarah also has widened her circle of friends by joining a nearby squash and tennis club. Club evenings there give them a social life unknown in Elmstone.

The street where they live runs between two main radial arteries radiating from the city centre. It is a quiet road, wide enough for cars to park without hindering traffic movement. The houses are all detached and have parking for one car only within their front gardens which means that there are usually several cars parked in the street. Occasional trees grow at regular intervals along the pavements. It is very much a middle class residential area with many families like the Wilsons but also many where the children have left the nest. In that case, the older residents are familiar with children playing in the gardens and are friendly to the newcomers. Having the two boys at the local school also helps integration because of meeting other parents at parents' evenings and when watching their children playing Saturday football matches.

But both he and Sarah miss the village community where they knew most people and were known, but at least in Norwich their friendships are not affected by the barrier between village priest and parishioner.

Chapter 17

The match on Saturday is the highlight of Victor's rugby year. Still in touch with his former club, he knows most of those who will be playing and this, he is certain, will add to the competitiveness of the contest. It won't be dirty play but it will be tough and rough – just what Victor wants and likes.

When the visiting team arrives by bus with some of their supporters, Victor is there with his team mates to greet them. Good tempered insults fly between them and the visitors are not slow in reminding Victor of his cassock and surplice performance of two years earlier at St. Edwards. Victor takes it all with a good grace but is determined to remember the jokes and harbours a determination to sort out the impertinent dogs on the field of play. With more time to attend training sessions at his new club, and in his new job, Victor feels in peak conditions and knows that there will be no possibility of a repetition of the previous incident.

The teams are very closely matched throughout the game. The lead swings from one side to the other with never more than a single score separating the two sides. Late in the second half, Victor's side is ahead by a single score of three points and is pressing for another try to put them out of reach of the St. Edwards team. In desperation the St. Edwards full back clears the ball with a kick to touch which takes play to within thirty metres of the Norwich try line.

The line-out which restarts play when a ball goes out over the sideline is one of the most technical aspects of rugby. The two sets of up to eight opposing forwards line up behind each other in two lines, side by side stretching away from the sideline but facing towards it. A player from the side with the throw-in then stands on the side line and throws the ball along the line between the two sides.

Victor's job in the lineout is first to listen to the pre-arranged call as to who is going to be the catcher. He then positions himself behind the catcher. As the thrower prepares to throw, Victor moves to stand beside the catcher and as the ball is actually thrown he and his team mate, gripping the catcher's legs and thighs hoist him above their heads such that he is now four or five feet clear of the opposition. Thus the opposition is fooled and the ball ends up with the attacking back division. Such is the theory.

However, as the thrower is preparing to throw, Victor suddenly, and to his complete amazement, catches sight of a face amongst the spectators immediately behind the thrower's arm. It is Alan. There is no doubt in Victor's mind. The two make eye contact and nothing could be more certain to Victor than that there is mutual recognition. He is stunned and, in a state of suspended animation - it is as though there is no one else around. Like a film which goes into slow motion during fast moving action sections, Victor goes into this phase. Unfortunately, it is Victor who goes into slow motion and the game which carries on at normal pace. Therefore, instead of getting into position and lifting the catcher, only Victor's fellow lifter is doing the lifting job. The catcher goes up on one side only and collapses upon Victor bringing the three players down to the ground. The ball sails over the collapsed heap of players, is caught by the St. Edwards player at the rear of the line out who seizes it with glee and heads for the Norwich line. He cuts between the scrum half and the fly half and runs for almost the full length of the pitch and touches down under the Norwich posts. The full back who should be a last line of defence is across the field hoping to make an extra man in the attack and the Norwich defence is left looking bemused. The try is followed by a conversion - and defeat is snatched from the jaws of victory.

As the final whistle blows, Victor runs across to the point where he saw Alan but there is no sign, nor did Victor expect to see him. Afterwards, in the changing rooms and bar there is much anger from his team mates and much laughter and ribaldry from his former team mates. The story of Victor and his clerical garb is much repeated to his embarrassment.

It is a match that Victor wants to forget as soon as possible.

*

"Are you sure?" asks Sarah later that evening.

"Yes, yes and more yes," says Victor testily. "Of course it was Alan and I've no doubt that he went there specifically to see me. I would guess that he didn't want to be seen and neither would he have been if it hadn't been for the coincidence of where he was standing at that line out."

"Well, why didn't he wait and speak to you afterwards?"

"Indeed. And equally, why has he totally disappeared from Elmstone. The answer must be that he doesn't want to be found."

"But you refused to take any action against him for assault and grievous bodily harm so he had nothing to fear on that front. So why else would he want to remain hidden?"

"It has got to be money," observes Victor. "He gave generously to the church but always in cash. Even when we suggested that we could get tax back on his donations if he filled in the necessary forms, he always said he would but in fact never did."

"And when his house was sold," remembers Sarah, "It was all done through a solicitor who steadfastly refused to give any details of his client or his whereabouts. Well, perhaps he'll turn up again."

Chapter 18

On the Wednesday of the following week, the family is sitting at their dining table after the evening meal. The dining table is an antique, inherited from a grandparent of Sarah, and is surrounded by a suite of Sheraton reproduction dining chairs. An old sideboard and a Welsh dresser complete the furnishings so that the room has a formality which makes for conversation. Sarah insists that, whatever else happens in an evening in the way of school activities and rugby training, Wednesday dinners are sacrosanct and are taken at the dining table. No television, and no mobile phones or similar distractions are allowed and civilised chat is required from all. Usually, any mail that has come in during the day is kept till all dishes are cleared away, the boys are usually in their rooms doing homework. But tonight there is only one letter and the boys are still there. It is addressed to Rev. and Mrs Victor Wilson and is a sealed package for which a delivery receipt was required. It is only with great self-control that Victor and Sarah refrain from opening it until the table is cleared. But now all is ready. Even the boys are aware of the intense interest in the package and stay to see what is in it.

With the paper knife Victor slits open the package and pulls out a small brown envelope in the manner of a conjurer producing a rabbit from a hat.

"Hey, Presto!"

"How exciting," says Sarah with heavy irony. "A brown envelope – fancy that."

Victor ignores the irony and slits open the envelope. Out fall two tickets. Sarah grabs one and son Roy the other.

"It's for a rugby match" shouts Roy.

"It's for the Scotland England international at Twickenham," squeaks Sarah.

"Let's have a look."

Victor takes Roy's ticket. "Unless I'm much mistaken, "he says," these are for the main stand and, I'm pretty sure they are right in the middle and just in front of the VIP box. They must have cost a fortune."

"Dad, Dad, can we go," shout the boys in unison.

"There's only two tickets," says Victor, "and I rather think they are meant for your mother and me. But I'll tell you what – all four of us will go to the next international at Twickenham if I can get tickets - and I think I can through the club. And how about going to your grandma's for the week end your Mum and I are away."

"Yeah," said with some eagerness. Going to Grandma means being grossly spoiled for the whole weekend.

"But are we going to go," asks Sarah, ever the voice of reason.

"Not go!" exclaims Victor in mock horror. "Are you serious?"

"But who has sent them? How do we know that there hasn't been a mistake. Maybe they are meant for someone else."

"Certainly not." Victor is quite emphatic. "We should regard these as being manna from heaven. Somebody somewhere loves us and wants to thank us for something."

"Someone back in Elmstone?"

"Perhaps. Perhaps we shall find out on the day. And if the boys are going to Southwold why don't we spend the night in a hotel in London and have a good dinner in the West End during the evening?"

"I'm not sure about the extravagance of that," responds Sarah. "I'll think about it." However, Victor can see she really likes the idea.

Two days later the decision is made for them. A letter arrives from a London hotel confirming the booking and payment for a double room for Rev and Mrs Wilson on the night after the match. Both Victor and Sarah are staggered.

"You didn't tell me you had a fairy godmother," says Victor. "But surely we'll find out who is behind this generosity."

Chapter 19

The match is still in its first half. Remarkably, Scotland are ahead and are camped on the English line where scrum after scrum collapses and has to be reset. The steam rises from the collapsed mass of sixteen rugby players is like that arising from a heap of manure. The smell from the heaving players is probably equally obnoxious being a combination of sweat and liniment. The crowd are on their feet howling for the English team to win the ball and clear their lines. The Scottish contingent are making an equal amount of noise calling for the referee to give a penalty try. Most of the people in the stand around Victor and Sarah are on their feet also. Victor is totally involved but Sarah is content to watch not only the play but also the spectators who are leaping around and showing more movement than is happening on the field. However, even she has to stand otherwise she is contemplating only the backsides of the spectators in front of her.

The day started early but has gone well. The early start allowed the family to get on the road at the unprecedentedly early hour of seven o'clock in the morning. They had delivered the two boys an hour later to Malcolm and Mary Porter who were, as always, delighted to see their grandchildren. They then parked their car in Ipswich and were able to catch a train to Liverpool Street station to arrive in London at half past ten. They had spent the rest of the morning walking round central London, finding and booking into their hotel in St. Katherine's dock. It looked very impressive and expensive. Next they walked to Westminster Abbey which neither of them had visited since they were children.

Then, by Tube and London bus, they headed for Twickenham joining the crowds of thousands including hundreds of Scots garishly dressed in kilts and "See-you Jimmy" bonnets. Clearly the Scots have had an enjoyable overnight train ride accompanied by a variety of alcoholic drinks. For the most part they are in good voice and, provided one could stand the volume, of no trouble to fellow passengers.

Victor loved every minute of it and, then, as they walk from the nearest tube station to the Twickenham ground amid the throng of spectators which gets denser and slower as they approach, he cannot restrain himself.

"Isn't this just great!"

"Once seen, never forgotten," replies Sarah jokingly. "Seriously, Victor, it is a great scene and it would be wonderful if you could get tickets one day and we can take the boys here."

Sure enough the tickets take them to seats exactly where Victor had predicted and they both enjoy surveying scene both behind and the seats immediately behind them.

"That's Prince Harry," whispers Sarah so as not to give the impression that she was interested in royalty.

"And that is the Wales coach right behind us."

"Where?" asks Sarah swivelling round and looking straight into the eyes of a bulky individual who smiles benignly.

"He seems a nice man," she whispers again.

"Appearances are deceptive," remarks Victor. "There are no nice characters at this level in international rugby."

The grandstand fills up. The players run onto the pitch amidst great cheers. As they line up for the national anthems, Sarah leans towards Victor.

"There's no one in the seat next to me."

"Maybe he'll turn up soon."

Finally, the England team win the ball from the scrum and the full back hoofs it into touch. There is a collective cheer mingled with groans and Sarah gives a loud scream. Heads, including Victor's, turn in her direction. Victor sees that Sarah is in a close embrace with a man in the seat next to her whose face he cannot see although he can see that the man has long grey hair. Finally, the clinch breaks and Victor sees the laughing face of Alan. They sit down and Alan leans across Sarah offering a handshake to Victor. Victor grins in response and takes the proffered hand.

"Nice to see you, Alan, even though you have gone grey since we last saw you." he says. "But you have some explaining to do."

"Later. For now, let's enjoy the game."

"Aren't you going to thank Alan for all today's arrangements?" demands Sarah.

"Like Alan said," says Victor. "Let's enjoy the game. Now we are here I'm going to see it with no distractions."

Come half time, the VIP box behind them clears completely - no doubt for alcoholic refreshment.

"Right, Alan. First, thanks for all this today. It is wonderful for us both and most of all it's meeting you again. Come on, let's have it – where have you been for the two years since you tried to bash my head in?"

"That will take too long for the fifteen minutes we have now. We'll go for a meal afterwards and I'll give you the full story. How are the boys doing? In fact, what are the boys doing?"

"Getting bigger every year," says Sarah.

"So I've seen," interjects Alan.

"So you've seen?" says Victor sharply. "Have you been spying on us?"

"Not at all. But I have passed your house occasionally and seen them. Scarcely recognised them."

"But why didn't you knock at the door?"

"Well, I thought it was too soon and perhaps memories were too raw. But your lads look great. It looks like you have got a couple of second row forwards in the making."

"Yes. At least I hope so. I think they'll end up taller than me."

"And you, Victor. How are you enjoying life?"

"I'll tell you everything – after we've had your story. Anyway, here's the teams coming back. Let's enjoy the game."

The match finishes with a convincing victory for England after Scotland fails to maintain the momentum they had built up in the first half. Sarah, Victor and Alan, along with the crowds, move towards the nearest bus station which then takes them into central London. Alan knows exactly where he is going and before long they are sitting at a table in a restaurant near Leicester Square.

Sarah feels grateful that she, instead of wearing her normal weekend clothes of T-shirt and scruffy jeans, has dressed up for the rugby match and the hotel. Not normally accustomed to eating in smart restaurants, she nonetheless accepts the treatment as one to the manner born, acknowledging with a nod and a gracious smile the waiter who had ushered her into her seat.

Alan speaks first. "Before I get into this, let's get a drink and choose what we want and then we can talk without distractions. If you are as hungry as I am, let's go the whole way with the four courses.

Alan summons the waiter. "A bottle of Pol Roger, please and the menus."

Victor looks at the prices. "You did say you were paying, didn't you?"

"Absolutely. And," raising his glass to each in turn, "long life and happiness to you both."

A few minutes are spent in silence, sampling the bubbly and studying the menu. The hovering waiter is summoned and orders are placed. Since someone else is paying, Sarah and Victor both go for a filet steak with trimmings. Alan orders rack of lamb.

"We'll have a bottle of Sancerre with the fish," says he, "and a bottle of the Chateau Lafite with the entrée. Does that suit?" he enquires of Victor.

"Come on, Alan," laughs Victor. "You know very well that we are totally ignorant on the subject. Chateau Lafite and a teacher's salary don't go together."

Alan laughs as well. "I think you will enjoy this,"

Soon, the starters arrive. Sarah has opted for a cold seafood platter with Alan and Victor going for lobster bisque. Once they are consumed, Alan clears his throat.

"Let me start," he begins, "by apologising for nearly beating your brains out in Sheringham and thanking you for not pressing charges against me. And I'm very sorry for ruining your life in the Church. I have followed what has happened to you since and I know that you were forced to resign from the parish at Elmstone."

"I think I can reassure you." Victor responded. "It may have been the best thing that happened to me. I've never been sure that I had enough commitment or belief to be a priest in the Church of England. My theology has always been a bit non-conformist and, apart altogether from the killing incident, I was being subject to quite a lot of criticism from within the congregation and the diocese.

"Now, I am happy in my teaching work. It is much easier to teach people to understand physics than to get them to believe in religion. For one thing most principles of physics you can demonstrate and produce evidence. You can't do that with religion. And, in fact, it's easier, right now, to talk about religion without preaching from behind a dog collar. And I am due you a much greater apology – I killed your son. And that is something I shall regret for the rest of my life. How can you ever forgive me?"

By this time, the fish course of plaice with a prawn sauce has come and gone and the steaks and lamb are approaching. With a flourish, the red wine is offered to Alan, is given the nod of approval, and is then dispensed around the table with appreciative noises from the diners. There is no hurry over the consumption of the main courses and Alan commences his tale.

"Victor, of course I forgive you. My son was a killer. In fact I have some gratitude for what you did. If alive George would now be in prison for the rest of his life. And, given my situation, that would give me great difficulties. Let me explain.

"I was a banker. Not a high street banker but an investment banker. My wife Molly died just after George was born and to my eternal shame I gave myself body and soul to the banking business which can be, literally, full time. I virtually abandoned George to a sister of Molly who didn't care for him. And that is where he went off the rails completely. I rarely saw him and when it was it was to criticise and try to discipline him. He went through a series of special schools for troubled children. Maybe he is a chip off the old block and takes his criminal instincts from me."

"Surely not," interjected Sarah.

"Wait till I tell you and you can make up your own minds. The thing about banking – at least the banking in which I was engaged – is that it has got nothing in common with the building in the High Street. That has an ATM on the outside and it is where you can negotiate, if you are lucky, with the branch manager for a loan to expand your business or buy a car. That's how it used to be. You put your money into the bank and you relied upon the manager to lend it out to others who need it. He would charge them for the privilege and be able to pay you a small interest amount. This left you happy because it was a lot better than putting the money into a box under the bed. And the bank manager was happy too. He had an income from the difference between the interest he was charging the borrower and the interest he gave to the depositor. It was a good deal for the manager since only he knew what the rates were. If he is giving a good deal to both parties, then he gets a good reputation and more and more depositors come to him. With a very large amount of money deposited, the manager can pay himself what he wants. Small increases in the difference between the rates can make huge differences in the manager's income. Soon he is earning much more than any of his customers. And he doesn't even need to be intelligent – just count up to ten! Multiply that by a few thousand customers or, in today's terms by a few million, then the amounts of money moving around are enormous."

Alan pauses and takes a sip of wine. "Projects the world over rely upon bank loans of millions even billions. Banks lend to each other to cover these loans and spread the risk and tiny differences in percentage points in these inter-bank interest rates, small in themselves, make massive profits to the bankers engaged in these trades. It is also possible to manipulate these rates for one's own personal benefit. Money is also made when bankers gamble on commodities and gambling is now an important part of banking. Most of the people dealing in this area are making large amounts of money by doing this trading as well as paying themselves vast salaries and so-called bonuses.

"When questioned, the bank bosses claim that they need to pay such sums in order to keep their skilled personnel. This is rubbish. The banks are full of clever men who would step into the shoes at half the salaries of the top men. This was what I did. I was in one of the banks which had to be bailed out by the government during the bank crisis of 2008. I was able to salt away quite a lot of money – loot, if you like – and get out before the crash."

Despite the distraction of Alan's tale, the meal is well advanced. Under the diligent eye of the sommelier, the first bottle of the red has disappeared and been replaced by a second.

"Was your money dishonestly earned?" asks Victor, conscious of the fact that he might be consuming something dishonestly earned but prepared to ignore any promptings of his conscience.

"Well – technically I suppose it was but it was commonplace if you knew how to do it."

"In other words – yes, it was dishonest," says Victor taking another gulp of the wine. Alan does not like this.

"All right, all right. But that's not the worst of it. The fact is that the life I was leading brought me into contact with criminal elements. One of the perks of the business was the ability to transfer monies from this country to foreign bank accounts in tax havens like Switzerland or the British Virgin Islands. One man in particular put me under pressure by threatening physical violence – disfigurement, knee capping. I knew he wasn't joking and I was terrified and really had to go along with him."

"Why couldn't you just report them to the police?" says Victor.

"Because that would have meant revealing to the police what I had been doing in taking out money myself. I would have gone to prison and he would have got to me there. So I took his money and transferred it to my own account in Switzerland and elsewhere and disappeared. And that was my big mistake. I chose the wrong man. This villain seems determined to hunt me down and has plenty of contacts to help him. If he does, it will be the end for me – and it won't be pleasant."

"Was all this before you came to Elmstone?" asks Sarah.

"Yes, that's right. I then reappeared in Elmstone as Alan Jones. You must remember that I always dealt in cash so that I could not be traced and why I was grateful to you for not pursuing me through the police. They would have found me and my relationship with George. I've had to do the same thing again and so now I have a new identity not unlike Alan Jones of Elmstone but somewhere I cannot be found. I'm building up friends – none as good as you both but I exist and with my wealth I give much to charity. That's why my life has to be as a lonely single man – but the alternative is too awful to contemplate. It's death or prison and, as I said, prison means death anyway. I promise you, I will not go to prison. I would rather die by my own hand."

"So there you are," he stopped and sat back in his chair."

"Wow!" sat Victor and Sarah together.

"When you struck me, were you actually trying to kill me?" asks Victor.

"I'm sorry – but the answer's 'yes'. As I followed you I was thinking about how the situation was panning out and I couldn't see a way out. I was desperate. If George was arrested I would have been identified and that would have been disastrous. I thought that he would probably try to kill you. Well, to be honest, I could see he was trying to kill you when you were on the beach. But I thought it more likely in a one against one situation that you would overcome him. In that case you would have guessed that I knew him and again my identity would have come out. Therefore the best outcome was that you both would die but, if not, you would be injured and that would give me time to clear out. As it happened, you killed George and I tried to kill you. If the landlady hadn't appeared I would have. But the main thing was that I had time to get away to another refuge, which is where I am now"

"And do you now wish you had killed me?" asks Victor. "And why contact us now? Aren't you putting yourself at risk should we decide to tell the police your story?"

"Because I have a conscience," says Alan ignoring the first part of the question. "I'm sorry, Victor, but I was desperate. I do feel bad about what happened although if the same situation occurred I would do the same again. But I now have a new identity, the chances of being discovered are remote. And I am sorry for what I did. Sorry it had to be you. I really enjoyed the company of both you and your children and, as I said, I trust you."

Sarah asks "What are the names of the persons who are chasing you?"

Alan hesitates. "I'm reluctant to tell you that. I don't want you to put you both in any danger."

"I don't see how knowing is going to make any difference," says Sarah. "At least if we do meet him we'll know who and what he is."

"O.K. The name is of the most determined of them is Ronald Machin and he is the only one who knows what I look like."

"Him and us, I suppose!" quips Sarah. "And by what name did he know you?"

Alan smiles. "Albert Johnson. Same initials and easy for me to remember."

"And why doesn't he go to the police?"

"Because that would mean revealing how he got the money illegally in the first place."

Victor suddenly comes back to reality.

"We promised to phone the boys and tell them how it's going and who the mystery donor was."

He pulls his phone out of his pocket and dials the Southwold number. The predictable conversation enfolds.

"Hi there, Gang. Yes, it was a great game. And guess who we met."

There is a barely audible gabble from the telephone and Victor looks amazed.

"You saw us!"

He breaks off and tell Sarah and Alan "We were on telly! Yes – there was a shot of the VIP seats and there we were - directly in front."

Alan has gone white. "Did I get that right – we've been on national TV?"

"Yes, apparently."

"Oh, shit," mutters Alan. "When did this occur during the match?"

Victor passes on the question over the telephone.

"Roy says it was at half time," he tells Alan.

"Victor, please stop the conversation and say you'll phone back."

Victor passes that on and puts down the phone.

"Look" begins Alan. "This could hardly be worse. There is every chance that I would have been seen by people I don't want to see me and even every chance that they would get someone to the ground who would spot me and follow me. Being with you would have protected me and they are probably here watching now. Don't look now," he says sharply as their instinct is to look around. "I had a look but I can't see him.

"I've got to get out of here," he says, "without them seeing me. There may be a way out through the toilets but I'll leave my coat here on the back of the chair. If someone approaches you tell them that our meeting was a chance encounter. There's no way I want you to get involved. I'm afraid I'll have to leave you with the bill but I promise I'll send you the money. I may have been picked up when we left the stadium and they are waiting outside now. Even when I have left you now, you may be followed out of here."

"What?" gasps Victor who cannot quite believe that Alan is serious. Alan doesn't even smile.

"I wouldn't put it past them if they think they could get to me through you. Look, friends, I'm going to have to run. Sorry. I'll be in touch."

He gets up from the table, drops his napkin casually on his seat and asks a waiter, "Where's the Gents?"

He then goes off in the indicated direction leaving his coat behind.

Victor and Sarah are staggered by this development but go through the motions of chatting normally. After about five minutes, Victor looks at his watch, speaks to Sarah and gets up and heads in the directions of the toilets. He returns almost immediately and goes through an exaggerated charade of gestures. Victor summons the waiter and requests the bill. While they are waiting a middle aged clean shaven man, well-dressed but wearing a light fawn quilted over-jacket approaches their table.

"Excuse me," he says. "I don't wish to be rude but can you tell me who was dining with you just now, please. I'm sure I've met him before somewhere and I was just coming to ask him but he has disappeared. Am I correct in thinking that his name is Albert Johnson."

"Yes, you're correct," responds Victor, looking him up and down and deducing that he had just walked in from outside. "It's quite amazing – he's left his coat here and also left us with the bill. As to who he is – he is a former parishioner of mine whom I haven't seen for more than two years. We've just met him by a strange co-incidence and even more strangely he's just left us with the bill but without even a goodbye. We can't understand it."

"And his address?"

"Just a minute," interrupts Sarah. "What is your name and where do you think you may have met him. "

"You're right, darling," says Victor. "Look. We've no idea where he lives and as I said, today's meeting was purely be accident. Give us your name and contact details and if he ever contacts us again, we'll let him know."

The man hesitates for a moment then takes a card case from an inside pocket of his coat. "Here's my business card. Phone that number and ask for Ronald Machin and they'll find me."

"All right, Mr. Machin. He may contact us to repay his share of the bill. If so we'll be sure to let him know that you would like to renew your acquaintance."

"I hope he does," says the man as he turns away from the table. "He's not the best man for paying his debts. You said he is a former parishioner of yours – you are a priest?"

"Yes," says Victor without going into details.

"Then I can assume that you are an honest man. In that case you ought to know that Albert Johnson is a dishonest man."

Rugby acquaintances of Victor would recognise that the set of his jaw indicates trouble but his discretion gets the better of him.

"Perhaps you are the dishonest man, not our friend." responds Victor sharply.

Machin starts to say something but stops. "Please just ask him to contact me" he says curtly and, turning, walks to the door and out.

"Ronald Machin – that's our man, I'm sure."

"Well, at least Alan has got away," murmurs Sarah, "although I don't think it was a good idea to antagonise this Machin character – always assuming that Alan is telling the truth."

"Don't worry. We'll never see him again."

"I just hope you're right. At least I will recognise him again in that fawn coloured coat he's wearing if he tries to follow us. Let's get the bill and walk back to our hotel."

As he unfolds the discreetly presented bill, Sarah sees his jaw drop. "Bloody hell," he nearly shouts. "Guess how much?"

"One hundred pounds?" suggests Sarah tentatively.

"I wish it were. Four hundred and seventy! Well, you can't say I don't know how to treat a girl."

After Sarah has raised her chin off the table, Victor pays the bill and they leave the restaurant pausing outside the door to look up and down the street.

"No fawn coat," says Victor.

"Assuming he has kept it on," says Sarah

"Oh, come on. You're getting paranoid. This is real life – not a crime novel," scoffs Victor.

Even in February the London streets are busy with both traffic and pedestrians and they stroll back towards their hotel enjoying the life of the capital. Not surprisingly, they fail to notice a figure in a black jacket but carrying a brown package under his arm following them fifty yards away on the far side of the street. He watches them into the hotel and then takes out his cell phone and calls a number. Apparently satisfied, he leaves and heads for the nearest underground station. An hour later, a middle aged couple book in for the night to the hotel and having gone to their room come down to the bar where they spend the rest of the evening.

Meanwhile, Sarah and Victor go to the hotel bar and have a small whisky and water as a nightcap. The couple who were in the bar have gone leaving them alone and finally they go to their room. There they luxuriate in a deep bath, large soft bath towels and a king sized bed and finally go to sleep satiated with food and sex.

Chapter 20

"There's one question which is really bugging me," says Sarah. "You've been aggrieved by the way you were treated by the Bishop after the George affair. You were never forgiven for your killing of George. So how do you feel about Alan?"

"Well, to be fair, the Bishop said I was forgiven but my actions could not be forgotten. But my view is — what is the good of being forgiven if it is still being held against me?"

"All right. Do you forgive Alan for what he did?"

A long pause from Victor. "Good question. No, I don't. Because it's obvious that although he is apologising now, he would do the same thing again. He said he was sorry it was me, but not sorry that he is prepared to kill to protect his true identity. I'm not even sure that he has forgiven me. He never answered your question when you asked if he regretted not killing me. What would have happened if he hadn't left so abruptly just now? Perhaps this whole episode was to get us into a position where he could kill us."

"Oh, Victor. Now you are being ridiculous," interjects Sarah.

"Am I really?" says Victor. "And it seems to me, and the bible is full of this message, true repentance is a necessary condition for forgiveness. Plainly, Alan doesn't repent for his actions so it is not so far-fetched."

"But neither do you repent!" says Sarah.

"True, but I did nothing criminal. And another thing!" Victor continues. "You must admit although we were friendly with Alan, we never really got to know him. We let him into our lives but he never reciprocated. We assume he was a good man because he gave generously, and was extremely amiable but that was probably a smokescreen to set up a personality which would give him some protection. Going by what he told us, he isn't a good man – certainly not an honest man. Basically, he is a crook. Only a crooked banker, admittedly, and they never seem to admit they've done anything wrong. Alan justifies himself by claiming that no one lost by his actions."

"Other than this Ronald Machin guy who feels very badly about it" says Sarah. "But then, if we believe Alan, Machin's money was ill gotten as well."

"If we believe Alan. It's a big if!" adds Victor. "So what do we do about him?" A silence ensues between them as they consider this.

Sarah and Victor are in the train coming back to Suffolk from London. Sarah had spent most of the night turning things over in her mind and during breakfast they had left the subject alone - the dining area being too public.

Being a Sunday morning, Victor was keen to go to church somewhere and so they went to an 8 o'clock communion service at a nearby church. Although disenchanted with the Church of England, he has not lost his faith which continues to draw him, somehow, to regular church services as a necessary part of his life.

After breakfast back at the hotel, they had walked to Liverpool Street station forgetting to look out for possible followers but, even if they had, they would not have seen the woman of the couple who had registered in the hotel after them the previous evening. She followed them to church for the morning service waiting outside until they left and now she is dressed in a mid-length dark orange coat, flat shoes and a close fitting hat. Having seen the pair look at the platform indicator, and then head towards platform 5, she went to the ticket office and purchased for herself a return ticket to Norwich, the final destination of the train Victor and Sarah were boarding.

Now she sits in the same carriage several rows away but out of earshot.

"More to the point," says Victor, "What do we do about yesterday and this person or group who, according to Alan, is trying to track him down? How do we know we weren't followed to the hotel and are not being followed now?"

They casually look around the carriage glancing quickly at the six people in it.

"Nobody there looks like they are looking at us." says Victor, "not that that means much. They all seem to be concentrating on their mobile phones or newspapers."

"Well, we'll lose them when we pick up our car anyway," remarks Sarah.

In Ipswich they leave the train and walk to the car park where they have left their car. It is a multi-story park some distance from the station and as they walk Sarah constantly looks around and behind them but spots nobody suspicious. They drive out, stopping at the gate to pay for the two days they have been there. As they drive up the ramp, Sarah half turns and looks behind their car. She sees a woman looking directly at them and they make eye contact before the woman looks away quickly.

"Oh, God," whispers Sarah in dismay.

"What. What's wrong?"

"That woman at the side of the ramp – I'm sure she was in the same carriage as us. She must have followed us here."

"Well. She won't be following us now."

Sarah is not satisfied. "But she will have our number. If she is with this Machin man trying to find Alan, they probably can find out who we are and where we live. So what do we do now?"

"Well, let's get to Southwold and pick up the boys anyway."

"Do you think that's safe. Perhaps we should leave them there till this is resolved."

"Resolved? Don't you think you're over dramatizing the situation? And how do we resolve it anyway?"

"Go to the police."

"And tell them what?"

"Tell them the facts."

"But we don't know the facts. We don't know who Alan really is. I don't think the police ever found out who his son George really was. So how can they tell what crime Alan has committed and against whom.

If you're right and the woman you saw has followed us and did get our car number and did find out who we are, it should simply confirm that we are what we said we were."

"But you're not what you said you were! You implied that you were a parish priest. And you're not. You're a physics teacher at a Norwich school."

"Well, that should be good enough to satisfy them. How many science teachers go to church? And at least we know the name of the man who is chasing him and also how to contact him."

In this mood, Sarah knows it is not worth arguing and no more is said about it until they have reached Sarah's parents in Southwold. The lunch and afternoon are taken with discussions of the rugby match and the meeting with Alan but the possibility that Victor and Sarah were followed on foot and in the train was avoided. Both are aware that to mention it would only cause quite unnecessary worry to Mary and Malcolm the grandparents.

So, late in the afternoon, the Wilson family set out for Norwich and home. The feeling of Victor and Sarah is the same. Being away is fun but coming home is better.

Arriving after darkness has fallen, none of them pay attention to a medium size, black saloon Ford parked against the pavement about fifty yards from their house. The Wilson's car is driven up a short driveway and parked at the side of the house just short of the garage where it will stay all night ready for a quick getaway the following morning since all parties must be off early for school or university. The boys who have fought most of the way from Southwold and have also fought over their mother's key, leap out and rush to the back door.

The house is cold and Sarah switches on the heating before looking at the floor inside the front door to see if any mail has been delivered on the Saturday after they left for Southwold. Her first thought is that there is a letter but as she approaches she sees that it is only a single sheet of paper folded over. Unconcerned she opens it but then gasps. Victor looks over at her to see what the problem is.

"It says," whispers Sarah. "We know where you are – now where is Albert Johnson? We shall be in touch." She looks up at Victor. "Surely this must be from Ronald Machin."

"I think that is a threat," replies Victor. "But how on earth did they find us?"

"So, what do we do now?"

"Call the police I would suggest. What was the name of the inspector who was dealing with Kirsten's attack?"

"Detective Inspector Barnes, I think."

"Yes, you're right. I'll call him right now."

Detective Inspector Barnes appears very quickly in response to Victor's call. It is the day after their return from London and he has come round in the early evening. They are in the main sitting room of the Wilsons' house looking out towards the street. The inspector's car is parked on the street just outside their front garden hedge. The boys have dashed upstairs and are busy in their rooms supposedly doing school homework; in reality the parents know that they are much more likely to be in communication with 'facebook' or 'WhatsApp' friends. The sitting room is not a room reserved for visitors. It is a working room with several books lying on chairs and a bookcase and two occasional tables. There is also a piano which Victor occasionally plays and this also is topped with a pile of books. Some of them are piano music books and there is an anglepoise reading lamp which is positioned to illuminate the music being played. On an open bookcase against one wall sits a large and oddly onion-shaped crystal vase which has been engraved with a picture of Elmstone church. This was presented to Victor on his departure from the parish. Victor is quite proud of it although Sarah would rather is was thrown out as she thinks it is hideous and although large its narrow neck is only suitable for a single bloom. Also, to her, it only brings the unhappy memories associated with their departure from there. There is a standard lamp behind a chair which is where Sarah does most of her reading. The chair is next to the window but facing so that she can see the street and all the passing traffic.

"The trouble is," says the policeman," that we have nothing to go on. There may be an implied threat from what Ronald Machin said, but it is not sufficient for us to take serious action. As I said, we can find no Alan Jones or Albert Johnson amongst any of the bank absconders who have been accused. Nor anything remotely similar of a criminal nature. And we totally failed to find him after his son's attack on Kirsten and his subsequent murderous assault on you.

"Since you didn't wish to pursue the matter we let it drop. Nor were we any better in finding out who George Meredith was. Father and son alike, both persons are inventions. Neither had a criminal record as far as we could see. No fingerprints from either of them are on record. If you had pressed charges against Jones we could have gone much further.

"Unless you can give us something to go on so that we can find Alan Jones ourselves, we cannot do anything. All I can do is give you my direct telephone number and I'll respond as quickly as possible if anything crops up. And this Ronald Machin you mentioned seems to be above board. The company referred to in the business card he gave you seems quite legitimate. But, again, without any criminal charges against him or his business there's not much we can do. He may well have money in various offshore companies or foreign bank accounts but they are legal as far as we can tell. But in any case that would mean that they are also outside our jurisdiction – more for the tax authorities than the police. He may also have underworld connections but, if so, they are unknown to us. It is the usual story. We need evidence to proceed."

"I know that situation," says Victor.

"There is one thing," says Sarah. "Alan left without paying for the meal we had. He said he would send it on, so if a letter comes we should be able to identify the post mark."

"Well, we are really clutching at straws now," responds Barnes with a slight chuckle. "From what you have told me of him, the chances of that are very, very slim. If you are correct, you might well hear directly from him. In that case, we can intervene. And it's not too late to bring charges against him for GBH or attempted murder if you wish. Again, you must contact me if you see any sign of anything suspicious."

D.I. Barnes leaves and Victor sees him out to his car. As he turns back into the house, he does not notice a curtain twitch on the upstairs room of a similar house to their own opposite to their own but about five houses further long the street.

After Barnes has left, Victor and Sarah look at each other, perplexed.

"I'm not happy with this," says Sarah. "If things happen quickly, there's no way we can get the police here in time."

"In that case it will be up to us," says Victor.

As they talk, the watcher in the house opposite makes a telephone call.

Chapter 21

It is Saturday, the end of the week following the meeting with Detective Inspector Barnes, and Sarah is sitting in her usual seat underneath the standard lamp which is on as the daylight has faded into dusk outside. On the table beside her is a writing pad and from time to time she stops reading, gazes thoughtfully into space and then makes some notes. Victor is watching television next door and both boys are upstairs doing what boys do when they are supposed to be doing homework. Both parents are of the same view - at least they are doing it quietly.

On the opposite side of the residential road, but some fifty metres further along, the watcher glances in the direction of the Wilson home and notes the lack of activity.

Suddenly, Sarah's attention is focussed on a movement further down the street where they live. There is a familiarity about it and when the figure passes a street light about fifty yards distant, walking towards them, she recognises instantly that it is Alan Jones. There is no car visible so, as far as she is aware, he has walked from the far end of the street.

In the house along the street, the watcher also notes the new arrival.

Sarah gives a short screech. "Victor, Victor! Here quickly!"

Energised by her tone. Victor appears almost immediately.

"What's wrong?"

"Look! It's Alan Jones. There's no car in sight so he must have parked somewhere nearby. I wonder where."

"We ought to find out if we can," says Victor.

"Victor, you answer the door and take him into the house," Sarah speaks quickly. "I'll get the boys to sneak out and find out his car number if possible. And I'll phone Inspector Barnes. If he's quick off the mark he might get here before Alan goes." She quickly leaves the room and heads upstairs to the bedrooms.

"James, come here quickly," she says urgently and ushers him into Roy's room. "Look, Alan Jones is just arriving. We need to find out his car number but he's parked somewhere outside this street. While we're talking to him, you both get out by the back door, go down the back lane and split at the bottom end so that one or other of you can follow him at a distance and see where he goes. And get the number of his car. And be quiet! It's important that he doesn't see you. Go on now."

She goes to her and Victor's bedroom where there is a telephone extension and puts through a call to Inspector Barnes's personal number. He answers immediately.

"Alan Jones is just arriving. Can you come?"

"I'm on my way. Hold him as long as you can."

Just then the front door bell rings. The boys speed down the stairs and through to the kitchen at the rear of the house. Victor comes out of the sitting room slowly and waits until the boys have disappeared. He answers the door.

"Alan! How wonderful to see you. I thought we had seen the last of you when you left the restaurant in a hurry. Come in, come in."

"Well," replies Alan, as he enters the house and follows Victor through to the sitting room, "I felt terribly guilty leaving you with the bill like that and without saying our farewells - so here I am."

"Sarah," shouts Victor, "Look who's here."

Sarah comes down the stairs and into the room.

"Alan, what a surprise," she gushes and ushers Alan into a chair with its back to the window. Standing at the door she asks "Now, how about a cup of tea – or would you like something stronger?"

"No, I won't stay. I just want to apologise for the way I ran out on you and to repay my debts. I still have to be very careful about where I go and who sees me. I take it you had no trouble after I left you."

"After you left us a man came to our table and asked who you were. A man in his fifties, medium height and well dressed. Looked more like a businessman than anything else. We just said that you were an old friend we hadn't seen for years and we didn't know where you lived. He said he thought he knew you as Albert Johnson. He gave us a business card and asked us to get you to contact him."

Alan gets to his feet, looks at the card and gives a mirthless laugh. "Ronald Machin. I did well to get away before he accosted you. That could have been nasty. But did anyone follow you after the restaurant?"

"Well, it's not exactly a situation we're used to – but as far as we could see there was nobody." Sarah is careful not to mention the incident with the woman who had followed them on the train from London nor the note which had been left.

"That's good. Hopefully I can relax a bit now." Alan takes off his coat and sits down once more.

"Where are the boys?" he asks.

"Out playing somewhere I think," responds Sarah.

"That's a pity. I hoped I'd see them as well."

Sarah goes into the kitchen and prepares a tray with a pot of tea and cups." She returns to the room and setting the tray down on an occasional table proceeds to pout tea. Alan appears to relax and the conversation reverts almost to the old times in Elmstone. They discuss the Elmstone personalities; Kirsten and her current happiness, the Derbyshires and others. After half an hour or so, Alan remarks "Well, it really has been nice to go down memory lane with you but it's about time that I was on my way," and stands up. "And I can't go without settling my debts."

He puts his hand inside his jacket as though reaching for a wallet when his attention is caught by a movement outside in the street. A car is slowing down and comes to a stop a few houses further along the street. The driver's door opens and he recognises immediately that the driver who gets out is none other than Ronald Machin. Machin comes down the street towards the house and up the garden path to the front door. He rings the door bell. Alan's first look of surprise changes to one of puzzlement. "How the hell did he know I am here," he mutters to himself.

"I'll go and see who that is," says Sarah and goes out into the front hall to answer the door.

"You had better come in." She turns and leads the way to the sitting room.

"Someone you know," she says to Alan.

"Well, well, Albert. Well met would you say?" Machin says. "You've kept ahead of me and my partners for a long time but it's come to an end."

Alan turns on Victor. "You bloody Judas," he swears. "You've betrayed me. What are your thirty pieces of silver worth? And you've been lying to me."

"No more than you've been doing to us." Sarah responds quickly. "You told us that Mr Machin is a crook – but that wasn't true. The police have told us that he seems legitimate."

"What lies has Johnson been telling you?" says Machin quietly. "He's just a common thief and a swindler. He has taken me for five million quid! And my partners have lost as much. He claimed he was an investment expert but robbed us and disappeared."

Victor says "The police checked on that, Alan, and Mr. Machin isn't guilty of any crime. But you are. And we've no idea how he managed to find us here."

Machin responds. "We followed you to Ipswich and got your car number. The rest was easy and the only bit of good luck is that I have a good friend who lives on a few houses away. I was coming to see you hoping that together we could find this bastard. But here you all are. And you, Albert, you're going nowhere until I hand you over to the police. I can document all your thieving."

"I told you to look for people following you," snarls Alan at Victor. "This is all your fault."

"No," says Victor. "Don't start that line with me, Alan. You are the criminal here and you may as well let us ring the police and have them come round. I'm sure that Mr. Machin here will be able to pin you down."

"The police," shouts Alan. "You've been discussing this with the police?"

"What do you expect? You played on our good nature and friendship but the whole thing was just a façade. And now you're doing the same thing again somewhere else. And living off your illegal earnings all the while. And I don't doubt that charade at Twickenham international was an attempt to get us on our own and then kill us both."

Alan Jones laughs. "Ah, well. Maybe I did. But now it has all worked out for the best. How very fortunate. I came here to find and finish off the job I started in London. You are two of the people who can identify me and pose a threat to me. Lo and behold, you've given me the third person in that category."

So saying, Alan pulls out from a shoulder holster underneath his jacket a small automatic pistol.

"The boys have seen you and can identify you. You can't possibly get away with killing us," shouts Victor.

Alan laughs again. "But they haven't seen me for years. And I've changed since then anyway."

Out of the corner of her eye, Sarah has now spotted another car entering the street and parking a few yards away. The driver steps out and she immediately sees that it is Detective Inspector Barnes accompanied by a second man. They start to walk towards the house. The bell rings again. Alan stops with the gun poised to shoot Machin.

"Come in, Inspector" shouts Sarah loudly.

There is a tentative knock at the sitting room door and Barnes sticks his head inside. Simultaneously, Alan grabs Sarah by one arm and thrusts the gun into her back. Barnes comes into the room and stops in the doorway. Machin backs away to the wall behind him and Victor moves to be close to where the bookcase with the vase stands within easy reach.

"Get out of my way." Alan spits it out.

"Give me the gun, sir," says Barnes slowly and quietly. "I don't know what crimes you may or may not have committed but murder will make your case much, much worse. Please, sir – now."

Victor butts in. "Alan, please do as Inspector Barnes says. What's the point of continuing?"

"You always were a pious pratt, Victor – and you're stupid as well. Do you think I'm going to hand myself in when I've spent time and money securing a safe existence elsewhere?

"I will not go to prison," he shouts. "Even if I have to shoot myself you will not take me. Now, I'm going to take Sarah, get to my car and get away. I promise you that if you try to stop me, Sarah will die. And that goes for the police as well. Don't try to follow me."

Then forcing Sarah in front of him he leaves the room pulling the door behind him. Just as he does so, Victor grabs the crystal vase and slings it with maximum force at the retreating figure. The vase catches the edge of the door and shatters. It is too late. Alan ignores it, drags Sarah out of the front door, onto the street and heads back in the direction he came from.

Chapter 22

"Here's Alan and Mummy," whispers Roy to James. "What are they doing?"

"Keep down!" hisses James as they crouch together behind a garden hedge.

Sarah and Alan pass within a few feet of the two boys. Alan is behind but close enough to be within touching distance. They turn the corner at the end of the street. A small grey car is parked some ten yards from the junction.

"He's got a gun!" James said quietly in horror. "What can we do?"

"They're getting into that car. We've already got its number plate."

They continue to watch as Alan ushers Sarah into the driver's seat of the car – a silver grey car with a ten year old number plate. Alan is making Sarah go in to the driver's side and then move across to the passenger side. That way there is no time at which she has got the car between him and her. He knows that Sarah is resourceful and that if she is to be a hostage he has got to keep her alive. Given half a chance she will try to make her escape. He is quite pleased to see that she puts on her seatbelt. If she does decide to make a break for it at any time this will slow her down and give him prior warning.

He quickly clambers in, transfers the gun to his left hand, closes the door and inserts the ignition key with his right. The key turns and the engine kicks to life. The car is automatic and he engages the drive with his right hand leaning across his body but keeping his left hand steady. Sarah is in no doubt that he is serious. The car moves off.

The two boys come out from the hedge and race back to their home. Their father and the two policemen are running towards them along the road.

"They've gone off in his car," stutters Roy breathlessly.

"Did you get the number plate?" questions DI Barnes sharply.

"UR16PMC," says James." It's an old Ford – kind of grey."

"Well done, lads." Barnes gets on his phone and issues an alert to all mobile police vehicles. "Approach with caution," he adds. "The male driver is armed and will be dangerous."

All three get into the police car and head off after Alan and Sarah.

"What about us," say the two boys plaintively but to deaf ears as the car disappears round the corner.

In the grey car, Sarah turns towards Alan.

"Alan, just where do you think this is going to get you?"

"Shut up, Sarah. You always did talk too much. But if you must know we're going to the airport."

"You have a plane? Or are you going to use me as a hostage to get one. Is that it?"

Alan does not reply. He is driving with one hand only but not taking risks. So far, there is no evidence of police cars following them and he does not expect any. He relaxes a little.

"Come on, Alan," Sarah presses. "Don't hold out on me."

"O.K. I have another car parked there. So I shall leave this one there and drive off into the great wide world where I have my current identity."

"And me? What about me?"

"Well, I'm safe enough at the moment since the police won't have seen this car or its number plate. I shall leave you in this car but I shall have to tie you up and also gag you to give me time to make my getaway. Don't worry. I shan't harm you."

Sarah is not at all happy about this. Alan has already indicated his willingness to kill to maintain his freedom and she simply does not believe him. Tying her up if she resisted would be fraught with difficulty and, in a public car park, well-nigh impossible. No! She sees clearly that in Alan's position to kill her would be by far the easiest solution for him.

Her best chance of survival is to bring things to a head while they are still moving and Alan's attention is split between her and driving the car. Alan speaks again.

"Please give my apologies to Victor," he says. "I was very nasty to him back there in your home. I didn't mean it. I guess it was the stress of the moment. And I have always enjoyed your and Victor's friendship and company – just sorry it had to be so shallow. All my fault. Also, by the way, if I don't come out of this alive I have left a document which will give you some facts and figures and what should amount to being a legal will."

"Where?" asks Sarah.

"You won't have to look far. It's in this car and I'll leave it here at the airport. And despite the various nasty things I've said to you, the fact is that you are the only people I trust."

"Thanks for nothing."

By now they are on the Norwich ring road which is a dual carriageway and goes within a mile or so of Norwich airport. Suddenly they are aware of a police siren and it is getting louder as it comes up behind them. A second police car then swings in behind them and stays there on the outer lane with its blue roof light flashing.

Alan curses furiously. "How the hell could they know this car?"

Sarah does not enlighten him. She decides that there and then is the best time to take the initiative into her own hands. The turning off the ring road towards the airport is approaching and Alan slows down to twenty miles per hour to turn into it. There is a signpost on the corner and just before they come to it, Sarah reaches across quickly, grabs and turns the steering wheel as strongly as she can with both hands. With only one hand on the wheel and less leverage than Sarah can apply, Alan is powerless to bring the car wheels straight again. The car hits the signpost and comes to a dead halt. There are no airbags, Alan has no seat belt fastened and thus hits the steering wheel with his chest as his head smashes into the windscreen. The windscreen breaks and the gun flies from his fist and goes out of the car through the broken window.

Sarah is restrained by her safety belt. She sees that the window frame has collapsed on top of Alan. He is unconscious. She decides to stay put until help arrives. There is a sharp pain in her chest. With exaggerated caution a policeman comes crawling to her door but keeping below window level. Sarah sees his back as he crouches and then his head appears above the bottom of the window.

"It's OK." she mouths silently at the policeman. And then gives a shriek of pain as the effort produces a sharp pain in her side.

The door handle is operated by the policeman and after a struggle it opens.

"Are you alright, madam?"

Sarah groans as the pain really hits her. "I think I may have cracked a rib or two" she croaks, "but apart from that, I'm fine". Then she faints.

"We'll need some cutting gear," someone shouts, "and an ambulance."

On the other side of the car, a second policeman struggles with the door but due to the force of the impact and its distortion of the bodywork, he is unable to do so. They wait for the ambulance and the Fire Brigade. Victor and Inspector Barnes arrive on the scene and Victor rushes to the wrecked car. He holds Sarah's hand as she slowly comes round to consciousness.

"Hold on, darling," he whispers into her ear. "The ambulance is coming." And as he says it, they hear the ambulance siren and finally see the flashing blue lights as it gets close.

Sarah is extracted from the car with relatively little trouble, given a shot of morphine, and, with Victor still holding her hand, she is taken off to the hospital. Alan is totally trapped because of the steering wheel and the folded bodywork and it is two hours before he is cut out of the crushed vehicle by the fire service. A second ambulance takes him off to the same hospital.

Chapter 23

"Bloody Alan Jones," says Sarah. "The last time we were in hospital I was visiting you and that was his fault. This time it's the other way round and it's his fault again. Damn the man."

Sarah is in a ward of the Norfolk and Norwich hospital. Victor is at her bedside. And there are curtains around the bed to give at least the appearance of privacy.

"He's a sad case. Imagine being in his position. He is on the run all the time, constantly looking over his shoulder and avoiding any kind of publicity. Remember his face when he discovered that he had been on TV. He was petrified with fear. I feel quite sorry for him. I shall certainly go to see him in prison."

"To gloat?"

"Come on, Sarah. You know me well enough. I don't kick a man when he's down."

"Not even in a rugby maul?"

"Only within the rules of the game."

The curtain round the bed is tweaked and the face of D.I. Barnes pokes through.

"How are we?"

"I'm very well, thank you, Inspector. My wife here is complaining that she wants to get home and is venting her frustration on me."

"That's what husbands are for. But I'm really here to give you a ticking off, Mrs. Wilson. You should have left everything to the police. You could easily have got badly hurt."

"I could easily have go shot," replies Sarah.

"But you were very courageous." Inspector Barnes finishes his sentence.

"And foolish," interjects Victor.

Sarah and Barnes ignore this.

"So it looks as if God looks after his own," remarks Barnes.

"More like – God helps those who help themselves," says Victor

"Or even – those who help themselves have more chance of success than those who wait for God to help," says Sarah.

"These subtleties of religion are beyond me." Barnes carries on "but we've been finding out a good deal about your friend Alan Jones or Albert Johnson and his son George Meredith. But whether we shall ever find out how much he has stashed away and where, we may never know."

"He said to me in the car that he had left a document somewhere explaining the what and the wherefore. He said it would be easy to find."

"Ah," says Barnes, "we have found a sealed envelope in the car and it's addressed to you Mr. Wilson. I'll give it to you now."

"I wonder what that's all about." asks Victor.

"I think I know the answer to that" says Sarah. "He said something to me in the car about a letter. Anyway, how is Alan?"

"Well, I can tell you one thing for sure. He won't be going to prison."

"What….." Sarah begins then stops. "You mean…?" She stops again as the implication dawns on her.

"He died" says Barnes.

"Oh, no!" Victor and Sarah are stunned. "How awful."

Barnes continues. "He suffered a major blow to his chest and they were too long in getting him to the hospital. But his blood pressure was very high and they couldn't operate until they got it down. It was touch and go for a couple of hours but he died just before I came in here."

"Oh, no," gasps Sarah. "That's my fault."

"Rubbish, rubbish, rubbish!" Victor speaks forcefully. "Don't even start thinking that way. Alan was determined not to go to prison and he was prepared to kill to avoid that. You prevented that at considerable risk to yourself. You always have told me that I shouldn't hold myself responsible for George's death. You have even less reason to blame yourself. It was an accident – pure and simple."

"I've no doubt that that is the case," adds Barnes. And I also have no doubt that you will be commended for your bravery. However, I have to say that having caused one accidental killing in your family is a misfortune but having two looks like carelessness." Barnes finishes with a little smirk at his quotation.

Sarah and Victor look at each other in shock as they recognise the source. Then Sarah starts to giggle, Victor joins in and they embrace in a mixture of laughter and tears.

"Oh, no," gasps Sarah in some pain."

"What's wrong?"

"Nothing much. It only hurts when I laugh." And they both start giggling again.

"I want to go home," says Sarah. "Now, please."

"Don't you want to see the contents of the letter we found in the glove box of the car?" asks Barnes.

"Does it concern us?" asks Victor.

"Very much so."

"Can it wait?"

"Definitely it can, but not indefinitely. And I'm afraid you have not seen the last of me yet either."

"Please." Sarah interrupts. I'm not able to cope with anything else to day. Let's just get home."

Two days later, Victor opens the envelope from Alan and is absorbing the contents. At the same time, a day in bed gets Sarah back on her feet and she struggles downstairs to the sitting room. She looks around.

"Hold on. Where is the crystal vase from Elmstone?"
"It got broken. I flung it at Alan as he was taking you away."

"I wondered what it was I heard. It doesn't say much for your aim. But since I've never liked it – it's about the one good thing to come out of all this."

"Well, not quite," says Victor. "The other news is both good and bad. Alan has left us all his wealth which is considerable and also the belongings of his son George since he was George's nearest relative. That includes several bank accounts, here and in Switzerland and a flat in Manchester which belonged to George and a house in Chester which was Alan's current abode. The one proviso is that we find out those to whom both Alan and George were indebted and make recompense. That is the bad news. The good news is that anything left is ours to do with as we wish. It's a poisoned chalice. If the fact that we were involuntarily the cause of the death of others has raised various moral issues, distributing millions of pounds of money will give us even more. And there is no indication of why Alan chose us."

"I can answer that," remarks Sarah. "He told me we were the only people he trusted. Well, at least we can get the cost of the London meal out of it," remarks Sarah. "The rest will have to wait for another day."

"Right," says Victor. "Let's drink to that."

"Is this God's will being carried out?" asks Sarah with tongue firmly in cheek.

Victor smiles ruefully. "You never know," he says.

The phone rings. It is D.I. Barnes.

"Have you come down to earth yet?" he enquires.

"Just about," Victor responds.

"We would like to stay in touch with you when you start to distribute the wealth you have acquired. We suspect that some odd characters will come out of the woods when it becomes known what has happened. Will you keep me in touch?"

"I'll let you know," says Victor and puts the phone down. He looks at Sarah with a hint of horror in his eyes as he realises the enormity of the task.

"God help us," he says.

THE END

Printed in the United States
by book printers

Printed in the United States
By Bookmasters